Andy Griffiths discovered a talent for crazy behaviour after accidentally sitting on an ants' nest. Since then he has alarmed the world with even crazier behaviour, including sitting on an ants' nest in the nude, sitting on a nude ants' nest, and letting nude ants sit on him. He has written three other books in the *Just!* series—*Just Kidding!*, *Just Annoying!* and *Just Stupid!* and has accidentally destroyed the universe and every living creature in it on at least three separate occasions.

Terry Denton is an illustrator. He gets to illustrate a lot. He is lucky. Luckier than if he was a builder. If he was a builder, he would hardly get to illustrate at all. If he was a dog, same thing . . . not much illustration. He has a friend who makes plastic things that fit on the ends of hoses. He doesn't get to illustrate at all. Not that he minds, because he loves making plastic things that fit on the end of hoses. He'd hate to be an illustrator. Terry, however, he'd hate to make plastic things that fit on the end of hoses. That's why he is an illustrator.

Also by Andy Griffiths
and illustrated by Terry Denton

Just Kidding!
Just Annoying!
Just Stupid!

JUST CRAZY!

ANDY GRIFFITHS

with illustrations by... TERRY DENTON

MACMILLAN CHILDREN'S BOOKS

First published 2000 by Pan Macmillan Australia Pty Ltd

First published in the UK in 2001 by Macmillan Children's Books
a division of Macmillan Publishers Limited
25 Eccleston Place, London SW1W 9NF
Basingstoke and Oxford
www.macmillan.com

Associated companies throughout the world

ISBN 0 330 39727 3

Text copyright © Andy Griffiths 2000
Illustrations copyright © Terry Denton 2000

1 3 5 7 9 8 6 4 2

A CIP catalogue record for this book is available from
the British Library.

Printed and bound in Great Britain by Mackays of Chatham plc, Kent

Contents

APART FROM MY PRESENCE,
EXPLAINING MY PRESENCE,
THIS PAGE IS ENTIRELY
   B L A N K.
ALTHOUGH THERE IS A LOT
OF STUFF OUTSIDE THE
EDGES OF THE PAGE THAT
I CANNOT REALLY SHARE WITH
YOU, BECAUSE YOU CANNOT SEE
IT. BUT I CAN. AND I'M ONLY AN
OLD CHICKEN BONE. YOU MUST
FEEL A BIT STUPID, BEING BETTERED
BY AN OLD CHICKEN BONE. EH!

Band-Aid

 ave you ever had a Band-Aid on for so long that you can't tell where the Band-Aid ends and your skin begins?

I have.

In fact, I have one right now.

It's been on for the last six months.

I've grown quite attached to it actually, and it's grown quite attached to me.

We've spent a lot of time together.

I did some calculations and I figured that I've had the Band-Aid on for one hundred and eighty-two and a half days, which is four thousand three hundred and eighty hours, or two hundred and sixty-two thousand and eight hundred minutes, or fifteen million seven hundred and sixty-eight thousand seconds or,

WHO WOULD EVER HAVE THOUGHT THAT THIS OL' BONE WOULD ONE DAY END UP OWNING HIS OWN BANDAID. WOW!

to be even more precise, well, I can't be any more precise because my calculator conked out when I tried to figure out how many milliseconds. There wasn't enough room on the screen for all the zeroes.

But you don't need to know how many milliseconds it is to know that it's more than enough time for a Band-Aid to get a very serious grip.

It's not my fault I had to leave it on so long.

It's Mum's fault.

If she didn't act like Band-Aids cost about three million pounds each, I'd be able to change them more often. She hides them and if I get hurt—no matter how bad—she'll only ever let me have one Band-Aid and that's it.

If I pull it off too soon and ask her for another one she says, 'Do you think we're made of Band-Aids? Do you think Band-Aids grow on trees? Do you think Band-Aids are handed out free on street corners?' And it doesn't matter how many times I ask her, she won't give me another one. So I've learned to leave them on. But I think I've left this one on just a little bit too long.

I'm never going to get it off.

But I have to.

Because we've got school photos today.

And it's on my face. Right under my left eye.

I can't have my photo taken with a Band-Aid on my face.

I'll look like an idiot.

I'll look even stupider than the year I blinked.

And even more stupider than the year the bench I was standing on rocked unexpectedly, and I opened my mouth in surprise.

If I have my picture taken with this Band-Aid on, everybody will look at the photograph when they're older and they won't remember me as the brilliant genius I was—they'll just remember me as the idiot with the Band-Aid on his face.

It's not fair.

I always get Band-Aids.

Everybody else has these really cool accidents where they end up with their arms and legs in plaster and they get all the sympathy and attention and everybody wants to sign their casts—it makes me sick. Why can't I get a proper injury like that? It would be so cool to break every bone in my body and have to

THE BANDAID FASHION ACCESSORY.

go to hospital and just lie around and watch television and eat ice-cream all day long.

But that will never happen to me.

If I broke every bone in my body the doctor would just look at me and say, 'He'll be right. Just put a couple of Band-Aids on him.' And then my mum would look at the doctor with her hands on her hips and say, 'Two Band-Aids? Do you think I'm made of Band-Aids? Do you think Band-Aids grow on trees? Do you think Band-Aids are handed out free on street corners?' And the doctor would say, 'Actually, you're right—one Band-Aid will be adequate.'

Anyway that's pretty much the story of my life when it comes to accidents. Nothing too serious. Not even the latest accident which *should* have been a lot more serious than it actually was.

I found this pair of glasses on the way home from school. Little gold-rimmed spectacles. Just lying in the middle of the footpath.

I would have left them there except I'd read a survey in the paper saying that most people thought people who wore glasses were more intelligent than people who didn't

JUST SERIOUS ACCIDENTS: Nº 36.

FALLING OFF TALL TOWER INTO DRINK BOTTLE.

ME, MECHANICAL BIRD.

4

wear them. So I had this idea that maybe I could make my teachers think that I'm smarter than I really am and they would give me better marks. So I picked up the glasses and put them on, but the lenses made everything sort of wonky and out of focus. The last thing I heard before I fell was, 'Look out!'

I ended up at the bottom of a roadworkers' trench.

But did I get a broken leg?

No.

A broken arm?

No.

Massive head injuries, complex fractures, amnesia and a nasty bruise?

No.

The only thing that broke were the glasses and the only injury I got was a cut under my left eye.

So much for glasses making you look more intelligent. I ended up looking stupider than ever.

But I'll fix that.

This Band-Aid has to go.

And today is the day.

I can't put it off any longer.

I grit my teeth.

HANDY RECIPES: NO. 6. BANDAID MUFFINS.

FLOUR.

EGGS.

MILK.

SUGAR.

...ETC...

YUM!

5

YOU, READER.

REMOVING A
BAND-AID
WITH NASA's
HELP.

I clench my jaw.

I take a deep breath.

This is it.

Stinging.

Burning.

Agony.

Pure agony.

More pure agony.

And I haven't even started yet.

Just thinking about it is painful.

What if my skin comes off with it?

What if I start to bleed and I can't stop?

And what if I just bleed and bleed and bleed, and the whole bathroom fills up with blood?

And what if I'm just treading blood and then my mum opens the door and all the blood surges out of the room like a tidal wave and picks Mum up as well as me and we go sailing off down the street and Mum screams, 'What's happening?' and I'll say, 'I just peeled my Band-Aid off, that's all', and she'll say, 'What? You peeled your Band-Aid off? Do you think I'm made of Band-Aids? Do you think Band-Aids grow on trees? Do you think Band-Aids are handed out free on street corners?' And I'll say, 'No, but they

LEG

POOH!
LEG FALL
OFF.

should be because then I wouldn't have had to wear the same one for six months and none of this would ever have happened!'

But you can go crazy thinking about stuff like this.

Better not to think about it.

I know what I should do.

Stop thinking and just do it.

Fast.

Get it over and done with.

A lot of people prolong the agony by thinking about it too much.

But not me.

When I say I'm going to do something then I do it. I don't just go on and on about it. I do it.

Really.

I really, really do it. Here goes.

I'm going to do it.

Right now.

Starting in a moment.

A moment from right now.

I mean right then.

Because in the time it took me to think this, right now became right then. And in the time it took me to think how right now became right then, right then became even righter then. And I can't start righter then

HOW TO PEEL A BANDAID USING ONLY ONE HAND.

1.

2.

3.

4.

5.

6.

7.

8.

TRY IT YOURSELF.

because that's already gone so I'm going to start right now instead.

On the count of three.

One. Two. Two and a half. Two and three-quarters. Two and four-fifths. Two and five-sixths. Two and sixth-sevenths. Two and seven-eighths . . .

REMOVING
A BANDAID
IN ANCIENT
TIMES.

This is not really working.

Better not to count.

Better just to do it.

Better to stop talking about it and thinking about it and just do it. Do it. Really do it. Now!

But first I need a pair of tweezers because the edge of the Band-Aid is so gummed down that there's nothing for me to grab on to.

I open the bathroom cabinet and look around inside it for the tweezers. I can't believe the stuff that's in here.

Baby shampoo, apple shampoo, anti-dandruff shampoo (that's Dad's in case you're wondering), hairclips, razor blades, a tub of anti-wrinkle cream (that's Mum's), sun-screen, cotton buds, pimple cream (that's Jen's—although if you ask me it's not working, in fact I reckon it's having the opposite effect), headache tablets, vitamin C tablets,

worming tablets (they're Sooty's . . . I think), a little container of weird-smelling ointment that Dad sometimes rubs onto his toes, about ten rolled-up tubes of almost-but-not-quite-finished toothpaste . . . Practically everything in the world except tweezers.

THE SAD STORY OF MRS TWEEZERS

20 YEARS LATER.

TWEEZER SKELETON.

And if you think I'm stalling for time by listing every single thing that's in the bathroom cupboard then you're wrong. I haven't even mentioned the perfume, the mouthwash—Jen's of course—the lipbalm, the bottles of nailpolish or the lipsticks. I could have mentioned these things but I didn't because I'm not trying to waste time . . . I'm just trying to find the tweezers.

I open the first-aid kit.

Ah! There they are.

I take them out.

Now I can get this Band-Aid off. Once and for all.

Except that the tweezers are a bit dirty. I should sterilise them under some hot water. You can't be too careful where germs are concerned.

I rinse the tweezers under the hot tap.

I suppose you think I'm stalling again. Well, I'm not.

REMOVING
A BANDAID
BY PIANO.

I'm not scared of a bit of pain.

In fact, I like it.

I thrive on it.

As far as I'm concerned, the more pain the better!

Sometimes, when I'm hammering a nail into a piece of wood, I like to hit my thumb on purpose . . . just to feel it throb. When I'm handling paper I always try to get a paper-cut because they *really* hurt. And I always make sure I lick my knife because tongue-cuts are even more painful than paper-cuts. But if you think that's bad, that's nothing. I've got a book called *The Encyclopaedia of Executions* and there's some stuff in there that's a lot worse than that. Like, for instance, there's people getting boiled alive, burned at the stake, and stretched out in the desert, covered with honey and eaten by ants . . . but all that is nothing compared to the pain of peeling off a Band-Aid that's been stuck to your skin for six months.

But it must be done.

And it's going to be done now.

The tweezers are ready.

I turn the tap off.

I brace myself.

1000h

10

ARM NOT
FUNNY.

I slide the points of the tweezers under the gummy edge of the Band-Aid. And start pulling . . . AAAAAAAGGGGGGGGHHHH-HHH!!! @%*!!!!!!!!@ @##**@ OUCH!! $!$%# %#$% @@ EEEEEEK!! #!!!!*!!!!! !!@@##**@ # YOW!! %&^%# #@!!!#@# $!$%#%#$%@ @#!!!!*!!!!!!!@ @##**@#!%&^%# #@!!!#@#$!$ %#%#$%@@#!!!! *!!!!!!!@ @##**@# AAAGG-GGHHH!!! %&^%##@!!!# @#$!$%#%# $%@ @#!!!!*!!!!! !!@@##**@#!%&^%# #@!!!#@#$!$ %#%#$% GRRRRRR!!! M@@#!!!!*!!! !!!!@@ ##**@#!%&^%# #@!!!#@#$!$ OOOCH! %#% #$%@@ #!!!!*!!!!!! !@@##** @#!%&^%## @!!!# OUOIU!!!! @# $!$%#%#$%@@ #!!!!* !!!!!!!@@##* *@#!%&^%##@!! !#@#$!$%#% UGGGH!!!! #$%@@#!!!!*! !!!!!!@@##** @#!%&^%## @!!!#@#$!$%#%#KHKJHOH!!!! $%@ @#!!!!*!!!!!!!@ @##**@#!%&^%# #@!!! #@# $!$%#%#$ %@@#!!!!*!! !!!!!@ @##* OUCH!!! *@#!% &^ %##@!!!#@#$!$%#%#$ %@@#!!!!*!! ·!!!!!@@##**@ #!%&^ %##@!!! #@# $!$%#%#$ %@@#!!!!*!!! OWWWW!!!! @@##**@#!%&^ %# RESTRSGFS!!!! #@!!!# @#$! $%#%#$%@@#!!!!*!!!! !!!@@##**@# !%&^%##@!!!# @#$!$%#%#$%@ @ #!!!!* !!!!!!!@@##**@#!%&^ EEEEEK!!! ^%##@!!! #@ #$!$%#%#$YOWWWWW!!! %@@#!!!!*!!!!!!!

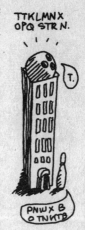

KLZSMPK!
OONZKT.

NKLP
TTWN.

@@　##**@#!%&^%##@!!!#@　#$!$%#%#
$%@@#!!!!* !!!!!!!@@# #**@#!%&^%## GFFG-
NEYTHGNS{A!!!　@!!!#@#$!$ %#%#$ %@@
#!!!!*!!!!!!!@　@##**@#　ZXZCZXZCV!!!! %
&^%##@!! @#$!$%#% #$%@@#!!!!* !!!!!!@@
##** #!%&^%PLKDVVVV!!! ##@!!!# @#$!$%#
%#$% @@#!!!!*!!!!! !!@@##**@#!%&^%##@
!!!#@　#$!$%#%#$%@　@#!!!!*!!!!!!! @IAARR?
I?I?!!!　@##**@#!%　&^%##@!!!#@　#$!$%#%
#$%@@#!!!! *!!!!!!!@@　OWWWW　!!!##**@#!
%&　^%##@!! !#@#$!$%#%#$%@@#!!!!*!!!!!!!
@@　##**@#!%&^%##@!!!#@#$!　$%#%#$
AAAGHHH %@@#!!!!*!!!! !!!@@## MMMNN-
BNBHHVG!!! **@#!%&^% ##@　!!!#@#$!$%
#%#$% @@#!!!!*!!!!!!!@@##**@#!%&^QW-
SQWQSWS!!!! %## @!!!#@# $!$%#%#$%@@
#!!!!*!!!!!!! @@##**@#! %&^%##@!!!#@#$!$%#
%#$%@@#!!!!*!!! !!!@@##* *@#!%&^%##@!!!
#@#$!$%#%# 　AAAGGH 　$%@@#!!!!*!!!!!!
!@@##**@#!%& AAGGHHH!!!! %##@!!!#@
#$!$%# %#$%@@ #!!!!*!!!!!!!@ @##**@#!%&^
%##@!!!#@#$!$%#%#M.ZSBVKHGDC;WKC
AJG!!!! $%@@# !!!!*!!!!!!!@@##**@#!%&^%##
@!!!#@　#$!$%#%#$%@@#!!!!*!!!!!!!@@##**
@#!%&^%##@ YIKES!!! #@#$!$% #%#$%@@
#!!!!*!!!!!!!@@ ##* * SDFACAVCA!!! @#!%&^%
##@　!!!#@# $!$%# %#$%@@#!!!!*!!!!!!!@@##

AZKLLPTW
OO BPTLK
NFL: 2G.

1000 W

12

**@#!%& ^%X WRTUIYLKTYUJRE!!!!#@
!!!#@ HUKLOLOIKM!!!! #$!$%#%#$%@@
#!!!!*!!! !!!!@ @##**@#!% &^%##@!!!#@#$!
$%#%#$ %@ @#!!!!*!!!!!!!@@##**@#!%&^%##
OOOOHHHH!!! #@#$!$% #%#$%@@#!!!!*
!!!!!!!!@@ ##**@#!%&^%## @!!!#@#$!$%#%#
$%@@ #!!!!*!!!!!!!@@##**@#!%&^%##@!!!#@
WOOHHH! #$!$%#%#$% @@#!!!!*!!!!!!!@
KFGSXKCHDGH!!! @ ##**@#!% &^%##@!!!
#@# $!$%#%# $%@@ #!!!!*!!!!! !!@@DLKOKI-
HJYHU!!! ##**@#!%&^ %##@!!!#@#$!$%#
%#$%@ @#!!!!*!!!!!!!@@# #**@#!%&^%
XXXXXCVBNM,NVCB!!##@!!!#@#$!$%#
%#$%@@#!!!!*!!!!!!! @@## ** PIWEYRG-
PQWYHCI!!!!@#!%&^%##@!!!#@#$!$%#%#
QEPIOURGHFP0WUYOUFJWPOFYVGO-
EUIDQERQWPEI7FTYN'!!!! $%*$^*%$*^$
SD;UB,JXVFXFDJDFSKDSU!!!! IDFLKDCG-
DNSDFXCZO!!!! IWRQOAXM,C;VBJHH!!!!
*!!!! !! !@@##**@#!% &^%##@!!!#@#$!$%#%
#$%@ @#!!!!* !!!!!!!@@ ##**@#!%&^%##@!!!
#@#$!$%# %#$%@ @#!!!! AAAGGGHHHH!!!

I have to stop.

It's the worst pain ever.

It's the worst pain in the history of worst
pains.

And I've only peeled off one and a half

millimetres. I've still got another sixty-eight and a half millimetres to go.

Maybe fast is not the answer.

But neither is slow.

I can't leave it on.

But I can't peel it off.

To peel or not to peel?

That is the question.

Or is it?

There must be a better way than peeling.

Peeling sucks.

It really sucks.

Sucks?

Sucks!

That's it!

Sucking is the answer!

I can use our new vacuum cleaner to suck this stupid Band-Aid off.

Our old vacuum cleaner broke recently and Mum and Dad replaced it with a new super-powerful model. It's so powerful it can practically suck dust off the surface of the moon. Not that I've actually tried yet, but I bet it could.

The Band-Aid won't stand a chance.

All I'll have to do is wave the vacuum cleaner near it and the Band-Aid will be off in a second.

No peeling.

No pain.

No nothing.

Just one quick suck and it will all be over.

I go to the hall cupboard and get the vacuum cleaner.

It's huge. I drag it into the bathroom and plug it in.

I take the brush off the end of the nozzle. I don't want anything getting in the way of its sucking power.

I switch it on. The noise is incredible. It sounds like it's powered by a jet engine.

I'd better concentrate.

It's a tricky job because I have to use the mirror to guide the nozzle into position. And the nozzle is so long I can't get as close to the mirror as I'd like to.

I guide the nozzle close to the Band-Aid. I can feel the Band-Aid lifting, but not quite separating from my cheek.

I go a bit closer.

Still not working.

I can't understand it. It should have pulled the Band-Aid free by now.

Maybe there's something blocking the nozzle. I pull it away from the Band-Aid and

HAND COVER
PAGE NUMBER.

FOR MORE INTERESTING FACTS ABOUT POWERFUL VACUUMS TURN TO PG. 96

look into the end. But I can't see anything. It's too dark.

I put it up closer to my eye.

And closer.

And just a little bit closer.

PHOOMPH!

My eye!

Help! The vacuum cleaner is stuck on my eye!

It's sucking my eyeball out of its socket!

The pain is incredible.

It's worse than paper-cuts, tongue-cuts, and whacking your thumb with a hammer all put together.

It's got to be even worse than being boiled alive, burned at the stake or being stretched out in the desert, covered with honey and eaten by ants.

HOW THE BODY WORKS: PART:7

EYEBROWS AND EYEBALLS

BRAIN

It's even worse than peeling off a Band-Aid . . . well . . . maybe not quite that bad, but you know what I mean.

And it's not just painful . . . it's potentially fatal.

It could suck my eyeball right out of its socket.

And my eyeball is connected to my brain. It could suck that out as well.

IS PAGE 16

Which would be even worse because my brain is connected to everything else . . . any moment now the whole inside of my body could be sucked out of my head!

I have to act.

Fast.

Now.

Right now!

I stretch my leg out and kick the 'off' switch. The noise dies down.

I pull the nozzle away from my eye and sit down on the side of the bath to catch my breath.

Right. That's it. Enough mucking around.

The vacuum cleaner is not the solution.

The Band-Aid is too well stuck.

I'm just going to have to do it by hand.

I grab the Band-Aid in the middle, pinch it as hard as I can and rip.

There.

It's off.

That wasn't so bad.

Hardly hurt a bit.

The trick to these things is just to get them over and done with as fast as possible.

I put the Band-Aid into my pocket—that could come in handy for annoying Jen later

on. She hates used Band-Aids. She thinks they're disgusting. Especially when they turn up in her sandwiches.

I stand up and look in the mirror.

It's amazing. Six months—and all that's left is a faint pink rectangle with a grey gummy outline.

No scar. Nothing. Just skin. Normal, perfectly healed skin.

Oh no.

I don't believe it.

The Band-Aid is gone and my cut has healed but now I have a big red and black nozzle ring around my left eye. It's sort of a combination of a bruise and a blood blister.

I can't have my photo taken like this.

What am I going to do?

Now I won't look like an idiot with a Band-Aid under my eye—now I'll look like an idiot wearing half a pair of glasses.

Glasses.

Glasses!

What better way to get my photo taken? Everybody will look at the school photo and think, who's that intelligent-looking guy with the glasses? He must be sooooo smart.

But I'm only wearing *half* a pair of glasses.

THEN COME PAGE 22.

I need to finish the job.

I know what I have to do.

It's going to hurt, but it will be worth it.

Like I said, I'm not scared of a little bit of pain.

I turn the vacuum cleaner back on.

It roars into action.

I put the nozzle up to my right eye.

Here goes.

PHOOMPH!

The nozzle grabs hold of my eyeball and starts sucking.

It doesn't feel quite as bad this time because I'm used to it, but still, it doesn't tickle.

I leave it there for as long as I can stand the pain. That should do it.

I turn around to hit the 'off' switch, but as I do, the vaccuum cleaner hose crashes into the open bathroom cabinet and wipes everything off the shelf.

It all comes tumbling off the shelves and smashes onto the bathroom tiles.

There's broken glass and shampoo and razor blades and perfume and soap and tablets and foul-smelling ointment all over the floor. And the vacuum cleaner nozzle is

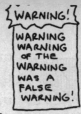

WARNING WARNING OF THE WARNING WAS A FALSE WARNING!

WHAT THE EYE SEES LOOKING UP A SUCKING VACUUM.

WHAT THE VACUUM SEES.

'BEWARE!' SAYS MS PATERSON OF VICTIMS OF VACUUMS.

ME SICK OF THIS.

still stuck on my eye. It's really starting to hurt now.

I go for the switch again but as I do I slip. I grab at the towel rail but all I get is a towel. It slides off and I fall down, hard.

OOF!

The right side of my face crunches against the tiles. I hit something sharp.

OUCH!

I lift my head.

I see a razor blade.

I see blood.

Blood!

My blood is on the floor!

And the vacuum cleaner is sucking my eyeball out.

I try to stand but I can't. My ankle hurts too much.

I can't reach the switch.

I'm pulling at the vacuum cleaner nozzle with both hands, pulling as hard as I can but I can't get it off.

I'm too weak.

I'm losing too much blood.

What a crazy way to die!

I drag myself across the floor towards the vacuum cleaner.

I push the 'off' switch.

The roaring subsides. The vacuum cleaner stops sucking.

I hold onto the sink and pull myself up.

I look in the mirror.

Oh no.

This is bad.

I have a big red and black nozzle mark around my right eye—it matches the other one perfectly. I look more intelligent than I ever dreamed possible.

But what I also have is a razor blade cut—just under my right eye.

It's bleeding.

A lot.

I'm going to need a Band-Aid on that.

WARNING!
WARNING
WARNING
OF THE
WARNING
WARNING
OF THE
WARNING
SHOULD
HAVE BEEN
A
WARNING
WARNING
THE
WARNING
WAS A
REAL
WARNING.

IS THAT CLEAR?

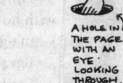

A DOT ON THE PAGE.

A HOLE IN THE PAGE WITH AN EYE LOOKING THROUGH.

21

YUM! HAND TASTE GOOD.

THE DOG ATE IT

'**Q**uick!' I yell. 'We have to stop him!'

Danny and I are chasing Sooty down the hall.

He's just eaten the model flying saucer that we made for our assignment on aliens. There's nothing left except a few scraps of chewed cardboard.

It took us the whole weekend to make that. We made it out of paper plates, egg-cartons and toilet rolls. It was painted green and had these little aliens sitting in the cock-pit we cut out from an egg-carton. Well, they weren't really aliens—they were two of Danny's toy soldiers but we melted their heads to make them look like aliens. It wasn't easy, either. We destroyed the whole platoon before we got two that looked exactly right. The flying saucer looked great too—just like the real thing. We just left it for a moment and then Sooty goes and eats it. I'm going to kill him.

Once I catch him.

He runs into the lounge room and scrambles under the couch.

'Get out!' I yell. 'Get out right now!'

But Sooty is not stupid.

Dumb, but not stupid.

RAFF.
RAFF

SCAMPER
LOVES TO
EAT
BROOMS.

He stays under the couch. He knows how angry I am.

'Ms Livingstone's going to be mad,' I say.

'I know,' says Danny. 'We're going to have to make it all over again.'

TRIXI LOVES
TO HIDE IN
THE FISH
BOWL.

'We might be able to make another flying saucer,' I say, 'but we can't make any more aliens. We don't have any soldiers left, remember? You wrecked them all.'

'*I* wrecked them all?' says Danny. 'You were the one who had the blowtorch up too high.'

MY DOG
FIFI LIKES
TO PLAY
IN THE
HOT WATER
SERVICE.

'Yeah, well, whatever,' I say. 'The fact is that we don't have our assignment.'

Danny shrugs. 'We'll just tell Ms Livingstone that Sooty ate it,' he says.

'What?' I say. 'Tell her "the dog ate it"?'

'Yeah,' says Danny. 'Why not?'

23

'Are you kidding?' I say.

'But it's the truth,' says Danny.

I shake my head.

'Danny,' I say, 'I know that and you know that, but to Ms Livingstone it will just sound like the most pathetic excuse in the world. Everybody uses that one!'

I'm not like Danny. I pride myself on my excuses. I may not get my homework in on time and I may not get the best marks, but I always have a good excuse. One that is original, brilliant and, most importantly, believable.

'Yeah,' says Danny. 'We need a really good excuse.' He thinks for a moment. 'How about we tell her your house burned down?'

'No good,' I say. 'I used that one a few months ago. Ms Livingstone already thinks we're living in a tent while the house is being rebuilt.'

'Why don't we tell her that the tent burnt down?'

'Danny!' I say. 'Get real.'

Danny frowns and shrugs.

'I don't know,' he says. 'Why would Sooty eat our flying saucer anyway? It was just cardboard and glue.'

'He'll eat anything,' I say. 'Horse poo, dead

24

birds . . . you name it he's eaten it. He even eats his own spew.'

'Gross!' says Danny.

'Not to him,' I say. 'He loves it. Sometimes I think he vomits just so he can eat it again.'

SOOTY'S STOMACH.

WE ARE IN A NEW WORLD, VO5.

JA MY CAPTAIN.

'That's it!' says Danny. 'Why don't we get him to vomit our flying saucer back up?'

'Yeah, right,' I say. 'That will get us a good mark. Ms Livingstone will be really impressed by a pile of frothy dog vomit.'

'No, I don't mean we'd hand it in,' says Danny. 'All we need is the aliens. We can build them another flying saucer.'

I can't believe it. Danny's actually had a good idea. It wouldn't be that hard to build another flying saucer. And we still have the written part of the assignment.

'I guess it's worth a try,' I say.

'But how do we get Sooty to be sick?' says Danny. 'Is there a command for that?'

'No,' I say. 'And if there was, Sooty wouldn't obey it anyway. We're going to have to *make* him sick.'

THINK VO5. WE ARE THE FIRST TO TREAD THESE PATHS.

'How?' says Danny. 'Force feed him dog food?'

'No,' I say. 'He can eat that forever and not be sick. Chocolate is what we need.'

25

'Good idea,' says Danny. 'Chocolate always makes me think better.'

'Not for us, you dope,' I say. 'For Sooty. One Easter, Sooty ate all my Easter eggs. A whole bag full. He was really sick then.'

'But where are we going to get that much chocolate?' says Danny. 'I don't have any money. Do you?'

'Relax,' I say. 'We don't need money. You stay here and guard Sooty. I'll be right back.'

I go to the laundry. Dad's secret chocolate supply is right at the back of the laundry cupboard. I don't know why we call it his secret supply, really. The only thing secret about it is that he doesn't know that we all know it's there.

I push the bottles of disinfectant and cleaning stuff out of the way and pull out a plastic bag full of chocolate. There are three bags of scorched almonds, a box of Jaffas, two family-sized blocks of milk chocolate, half a dozen caramel Easter eggs and a big tray of assorted creams. If that doesn't make him sick, then nothing will.

I take the bag into the lounge room.

'Here, Sooty,' I call. I unwrap a caramel nut swirl. I crunch the wrapper noisily in my hand.

That ought to do the trick. Sooty can never resist the sound of food being opened.

He pokes his head out from under the couch.

I wave the chocolate under his nose.

'Look, Sooty,' I say. 'Caramel nut swirl!'

Sooty wriggles the rest of his body out from under the couch, but he doesn't take the bait.

He just stands and looks at me. Maybe he's too full of flying saucer. Or maybe he remembers how much trouble he got in the time he ate all my Easter eggs.

I bite the caramel nut swirl in half.

'Mmmm,' I say. 'Yummy. Want a bite of this hand-picked peanut dipped in caramel and smothered in rich dark chocolate, Sooty? It's delicious.'

I don't know about Sooty, but it's working on Danny. He's practically drooling all over the carpet.

'Can I have one?' he says.

'Just one,' I say. 'Keep the rest for Sooty.'

Danny picks one up and unwraps it.

I put mine under Sooty's nose.

'You know you want it,' I say. 'So have it! You deserve it.'

WE CALL THIS NEW LAND, ZOGLAND.

JA

Sooty sniffs it. He licks it and takes it into his mouth and swallows it whole. He doesn't need any more encouragement. He starts wolfing down chocolates as fast as Danny and I can unwrap them. Every now and again we have one as well. Well, to tell you the truth, it's hard to tell who's eating the most—Sooty or us. Danny has chocolate all around his mouth—it's dribbling down his chin onto his shirt.

Suddenly the door opens.

'Andy!' says Dad. 'What do you think you're doing?!'

I look up. Dad is home early.

'Dad!' I say. 'I didn't expect you home this early!'

I'M JUST CRAZY

'Obviously not,' he says. He bends down and picks up a chocolate wrapper. 'Have you been eating my chocolates?'

'No, Dad . . .' I say. 'It was Sooty! I came in here and they were everywhere.'

I point at Sooty.

'Bad dog!' I say. 'You're a very bad dog!'

Dad shakes his head. 'Andy, do you really expect me to believe that?'

'Yes,' I say.

'But it's all over your face,' says Dad. 'And Danny's too.'

1000M

28

Danny quickly pulls up his T-shirt and wipes his face. But there's so much chocolate on his shirt that it only makes it worse.

'Um, yes,' I say, 'that's true. But we just wanted to make sure that the chocolate hadn't passed its use-by date . . . in case we had to take Sooty to hospital.'

'Yeah,' says Danny. 'Can't be too careful with use-by dates.'

I think it's quite a good excuse, but Dad is not listening. He is beyond listening. He is getting ready to give a lecture.

'Andy,' he says, 'it's bad enough that you steal my chocolate.'

'Yes, Dad.'

When Dad is lecturing I find it's best to just agree with everything he says. It seems to calm him down.

'And it's even worse that you compound your crime by eating my chocolate.'

'Yes, Dad.'

'But then to waste it on the dog—that is really stupid!'

'Yes, Dad.'

'And then to *blame* the poor dog!'

'Yes, Dad.'

'Do you really expect me to believe that he

29

went into the laundry, opened the cupboard door, pulled the chocolates out, carried them to the lounge room and unwrapped them all by himself? What do you take me for—an idiot?'

'Yes, Dad.'

'What!?'

Oops. Sometimes it's better not to agree.

'I mean, no, Dad.'

Now he's *really* mad.

'Clean up this mess,' he says. 'And you can replace what you have eaten out of your own pocket money.'

'Yes, Dad.'

He turns and leaves the room.

I look at Sooty.

'This is your fault,' I say.

'Yeah,' says Danny. 'It's all your fault.'

Sooty just sits down and scratches himself. He doesn't care.

'The least you could do is be sick!' I say.

He stares back at me.

'Come on, Sooty!' I say. 'Be sick!'

'It's not working,' says Danny.

Suddenly I have a brainwave. I'm not a smoker or anything, but I did have a puff once. I was with my cousin, David. He said I should learn to smoke because it really

impresses girls. But I didn't impress anybody. All I did was cough so much that I was sick. If I can get Sooty to smoke a cigarette then maybe it will have the same effect on him.

'It doesn't matter,' I say to Danny. 'I've got a better idea. Let's make him smoke.'

'Is he old enough?' says Danny.

'He is in dog years,' I say. 'Come on.'

I grab Sooty by the collar, drag him outside and lock him underneath the house.

'Wait there,' I say. 'We'll be back in a minute.'

We go out into the street and search the nature strip for butts. We find a couple and go back under the house. It's very cramped and dark and we have to double over.

I find a box of barbecue matches and light one of the butts. I suck the smoke back.

It tastes horrible. I cough so hard I almost throw up. Perfect!

I offer the butt to Sooty but he turns his head away. I try to put it in his mouth but he just keeps moving his head from side to side.

'Come on, Sooty,' I wheeze. 'Think how cool you'll look when you learn to smoke. And how tough. The girl dogs will all go for you for sure.'

MORE SOTTY THE WOODER DOO

THE ENK.

31

'Isn't this a bit cruel?' says Danny. 'I mean, won't it stunt his growth?'

'He's short already,' I say. 'He can hardly get any shorter.'

'But what if he gets hooked?' says Danny.

'Then we'll ring the Quit line,' I say. 'But first we'll get our aliens back.'

But Sooty has other ideas. He jerks his head away from me and knocks the butt out of my hands. It falls into my lap.

'Ahhhh!' I scream. I jump up.

WHACK!

My head hits the roof.

'Ouch!' I yell.

'Andy?' calls Mum. 'Is that you under there?'

'No, Mum,' I say, hoping that she will believe me and go away.

'Are you smoking?'

'No,' I say.

'Then why can I smell smoke?' she says.

'It's Sooty,' I say. 'We're trying to get him to stop but he won't listen.'

'Andy, get out here this minute!' says Mum.

We all crawl out.

Mum is standing there with her hands on her hips.

32

'That's the most pathetic excuse I've ever heard,' she says. 'When are you going to grow up and start taking responsibility for your actions?'

'But, Mum . . .' I say.

'No, listen to me,' says Mum. 'I know you think it looks cool, and tough, and that it will make girls like you, but do you realise what smoking can do to your health?'

'But . . .' I say.

'It rots your lungs. It stunts your growth. It ruins your circulation. You'll get gangrene and your toes will drop off. Is that what you want?'

'Are you getting all this, Sooty?' I say.

'I'm talking to you!' says Mum. 'You two would be a lot better off playing outside in the fresh air than huddled under the house smoking. Why don't you go to the playground? The exercise would do you good.'

The playground? How old does she think we are?

'But, Mum,' I say, 'playgrounds are for kids.'

'Don't be silly,' says Mum. 'Playgrounds are for everybody.'

'Why don't *you* go down there then?' I say.

'Well,' says Mum, 'because at my age swings and seesaws and whizzy-dizzys make me feel ill, but if I was your age I'd be down there in a flash.'

I look at Danny.

Danny looks at me.

'That's it!' I say. 'Great idea, Mum! Can we take Sooty?'

'Sure,' says Mum, a little surprised by my sudden change of mind. 'But no more smoking!'

'Okay,' I say. 'Did you hear that, Sooty? No more smoking!'

Mum rolls her eyes.

We grab Sooty and drag him down the driveway, across the street and down to the playground.

'This ought to do the trick,' I say to Danny. 'Chocolate, smoking and swinging—a lethal combination. Even for a dog with a cast-iron gut like Sooty.'

Sooty digs his claws into the footpath the whole way. Sometimes I swear he can understand English. I have to drag him by the collar while Danny pushes him along from behind.

Finally we make it to the playground.

34

'Gee,' says Danny. 'This place has changed.'

He's right. The playground is not what it used to be. They've removed all the old metal stuff we used to play on and replaced it with a load of brightly coloured plastic junk. It's strictly for babies. There are still swings but they're not the big ones—just the ones that look like rubber underpants with little safety chains across the front. Still, they'll be perfect for Sooty.

FUN WITH RUBBER UNDERPANTS.

STRETCH THEM.

He's not too keen on the idea, though. He's straining to get away.

'Don't worry, Sooty,' I say. 'We're not mad at you. We're just going to have a bit of fun.'

I try to pick him up, but he's twisting and turning and I can't get a proper grip.

'Give me a hand, Danny,' I say.

INFLATE THEM WITH GAS.

But Danny is not beside me. I look up. He's climbing across the top of a yellow dome.

'Hey!' he calls. 'Your mum was right. This is pretty good! We should come here more often.'

FLOAT AWAY ON THEM

'Danny!' I yell. 'Get over here right now! Don't you realise what's at stake?'

'Just one more go?' he says.

'Danny!'

Danny jumps off the dome and comes running over.

I put my hands around Sooty's chest and hold him just above the swing. As I lower him into the rubber seat, Danny pulls Sooty's hind legs through the legholes. I pull the chain across and lock it into position.

I run around behind the swing, pull it back and push it as hard as I can.

Sooty goes swinging up into the air. He barks crazily. The swing comes whooshing back and I push it even harder. He barks even louder.

'Hey!' says a voice behind us. 'Take that dog out of there!'

I turn around.

It's my neighbour, Mr Broadbent. He doesn't like me very much. I think it's got something to do with the time I accidentally set his fence on fire.

'Let him go!' he says.

'But Sooty likes it,' I say. 'He just loves the swing.'

'Then why is he barking like that?' says Mr Broadbent.

'He's barking for joy,' I say, giving the swing another push. All I've got to do is to

keep Mr Broadbent talking. A couple more swings should do it. Just a couple more.

'If you don't let that dog out of there I'm going to ring the RSPCA,' says Mr Broadbent.

'Actually, it's the RSPCA who told me to do this,' I say. 'They said swinging is good for dogs. It makes them mentally happy. You should try it.'

'I don't have a dog,' he says.

'I meant for you,' I say.

I push Sooty again.

'Are you going to stop that or do I have to come over there and make you?' says Mr Broadbent.

'Just one more and I'm through,' I say.

I give Sooty one last big push.

Sooty flies up, up, up into the air.

But he doesn't come back down again.

He keeps going.

He flies out of the swing like he's been shot out of a cannon. He travels across the park and lands out of sight behind some trees.

Mr Broadbent shakes his head.

'That poor dog,' he says.

'How could I know that was going to happen?' I say. 'This playground equipment is dangerous. The seatbelts are hopeless!'

WHEN AN OLD VACUUM DIES, ITS MATE WILL STAY WITH THE BODY FOR MONTHS, HOWLING AT THE MOON.

I grab Danny.

'Come on,' I say. 'We have to catch him. He could spew at any moment!'

We run towards the trees.

We find Sooty walking around and around the base of a large pine tree.

'There he is!' says Danny. 'Looks like he's going to be sick.'

'Shush,' I say. 'I don't want him to know we're here. He might run off.'

We hide behind a park bench and watch him.

Sooty circles the tree.

Then he stops.

Maybe the combination of chocolate, smoke, swinging and flying through the air has done the trick. He's finally going to be sick.

But Sooty doesn't throw up. He lifts his leg and wees on the tree trunk.

Danny giggles.

'Having fun, boys?' says a voice behind us.

I turn around.

Oh no.

I'm staring at a big slobbering Rottweiler. I look up.

It's Roseanne O'Reilly . . . and Lisa

38

Mackney. They must be taking Roseanne's Rottweiler for a walk.

Roseanne turns to Lisa.

'Spying on a dog having a wee is kind of pathetic, don't you think?' she says.

'No,' says Lisa. 'It's not kind of pathetic. It's definitely pathetic.'

'No, you don't understand,' I say. 'I can explain . . .'

'Yeah,' says Danny. 'We didn't want to watch him having a wee. We were hoping he was going to be sick.'

Lisa and Roseanne look horrified.

'That's even worse,' says Roseanne. 'Come on, Lisa. Let's get away from these psychos.'

They walk off. Lisa looks sadly back at me over her shoulder.

Damn. Of all the parks she could have come into, why did she have to come into this one? And why right now? I want to run after her and explain, but I can't leave Sooty. Stupid dog. This is all his fault.

Roseanne calls to her Rottweiler.

He's over at the tree sniffing at the place where Sooty just lifted his leg.

Uh-oh.

They start growling and circling each

GOSH, I'LL HAVE TO TRY IT.

HOW TIME FLIES.

other. The hairs rise into spiky patterns on their backs.

The Rottweiler lunges at Sooty and sinks his teeth into Sooty's throat.

'No, Slayer!' screams Roseanne.

I jump up and run towards them.

I grab Sooty by the tail and pull him up into the air. But Slayer comes too, still attached to Sooty's neck.

For a moment I'm holding both dogs in the air, but then Slayer loses his grip and falls to the ground. He jumps back up and snaps at Sooty.

I swing Sooty away from him, but he follows, lunging and snapping. I have to keep swinging Sooty around and around and around.

'Do something, Roseanne!' screams Lisa.

'No, Slayer,' calls Roseanne again. 'Bad dog!'

'Go, Andy!' yells Danny.

'Do something, Danny!' I scream.

Danny picks up a pine cone and throws it at Slayer.

It hits me in the head. Ouch! Right where I bumped it earlier under the house.

'Sorry!' says Danny.

He tries again. This one is a better shot. It hits Slayer in the side.

Slayer stops trying to bite Sooty and starts trying to bite me instead.

He sinks his teeth into my leg.

'Aaggh!' I yell.

I drop Sooty.

Sooty sprints away towards home.

'Quick, Danny!' I yell.

I try to run after Sooty but I'm dizzy from spinning around and I run into a tree.

Ouch.

Danny helps me up.

Lisa and Roseanne are just standing there shaking their heads and laughing.

I want to tell Roseanne off for not keeping her crazy dog on a leash but I don't have time for that now. We have to catch Sooty.

Danny and I take off after him. We chase him all the way home.

When we get there, Sooty is in the backyard, lying on the grass, panting.

(ANDY SHOULD BE PUT DOWN.)(T.D.)

(TERRY SHOULD BE PUT DOWN) (Andy.)

Danny and I flop down beside him.

'Poor dog,' says Danny. 'Look at him. He's exhausted.'

I said it fiVst! (T.D)

Poor dog? What about me? I've been blasted by Dad, lost at least ten weeks' pocket money,

WHO CAReS! (Andy.)

41

PRETTY FUNNY?

whacked my head, been blasted by Mum, been humiliated in front of Lisa, hit by a pine cone, bitten by a dog and had a head-on with a tree. And Sooty still hasn't been sick. It's not fair.

'What now?' says Danny.

'I hate to say it,' I say, 'but I think we're going to have to tell Ms Livingstone the truth.'

'But you said . . .' says Danny. 'You said . . .'

CLOSE-UP ON DOG VOMIT.

PIECE OF DUG-UP, RECENTLY DEAD, PET RABBIT.

CAT FUR

PIECES OF BROCCOLI FED TO IT FROM LAST NIGHT'S DINNER

PIECE OF PAPER BOY'S LEG

'I know, Danny,' I say. 'But that was before we'd tried everything. He's not going to spew. The only thing left is to wait until it comes out the other end, and there's no way I'm going to touch that.'

'Hang on,' says Danny, grabbing my arm so hard it hurts. 'Look!'

He's pointing towards Sooty.

I don't believe it.

Sooty's wandered to the edge of the lawn and is being sick.

It's the most wonderful thing I've ever seen!

'Good dog, Sooty,' I say. 'Bring it all up. You'll feel better.'

He coughs a few more times and walks away.

'Come on, Danny,' I say. 'We've got work to do.'

We go over and kneel beside the pile of

42

OF COURSE ALL MY MECHANICAL BIRD FRIENDS THINK...

steaming, frothy goo. It's a yellowy sort of colour with patches of brown.

I grab a stick and start poking at it, looking for the flying saucer.

Danny does the same.

I find a piece of what I think is our assignment, but on closer examination it turns out to be part of a chocolate wrapper.

Searching through Sooty's vomit with a stick is not exactly my idea of a great afternoon's entertainment. But what's really bad is that there's no trace of the flying saucer. Or the aliens.

I push aside another lump of half-chewed chocolate and then I see something green. There they are! Our aliens!

'Danny!' I say. 'I found them!'

Danny stares down into Sooty's sick and smiles widely.

'I bet those guys are pleased to see us,' he says.

'EEERRRGGHHH! I don't believe you two!' says a voice behind us.

I turn around. It's Jen.

'You are gross!' she says. 'I've never heard of anyone weird enough to play with their own sick!'

THINGS TO BE FOUND IN A NORMAL PILE OF DOG VOMIT.

FLUFFY'S COLLAR.

DING!
FLUFFY'S BELL.

WHY ME!
STING

THE QUEEN MOTHER

FLUFFY

43

THAT THE PICTURES ARE THE BEST BIT.

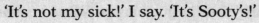

HOW TO MAKE YOUR DOG SICK.

MAKE HIM SLEEP IN YOUR UNDERPANTS' DRAWER.

BLEACH

PUT YOUR SOCKS OVER ITS NOSE.

TELL IT YOUR LIFE STORY.

'It's not my sick!' I say. 'It's Sooty's!'

'I'm going to tell Mum,' she says, putting her hand up to her mouth. 'You two need help. Serious professional help!'

Jen turns and starts to run.

I'm already in enough trouble. I don't really think Mum needs to know about this.

'Quick, Danny,' I say. 'Help me stop her!'

We get up and run after her. I grab Jen's shoulder.

'Get your spewy hands off me!' she screams. She shakes us off and runs up the steps into the house.

'That's all I need,' I say, turning back to Danny. 'But at least we found the aliens.'

'Oh no,' says Danny, 'look!'

Sooty has returned to his vomit. And he's eating it like he hasn't eaten for a week.

'Get away from that, you crazy dog!' I scream.

We run over to scare him away, but it's too late. They've gone. He's eaten them.

Again.

'You stupid dog!' I yell. 'You ate our aliens! Twice! I'm going to kill you!'

I put my hands around his throat and start to squeeze.

THE STORIES ARE OK. BUT THE DRAWINGS ARE SOOO FUNNY.

'Andy!' says Mum sharply. 'What is wrong with you today?'

She's standing outside the back door.

I let Sooty go.

'Nothing, Mum,' I say.

'Nothing?' she says. 'Your father told me about the chocolate. And Mr Broadbent has just been on the phone telling me what you were doing to Sooty in the playground. Then Jen comes in and says you were sick and she saw you playing with it. And now I find you strangling the poor dog.'

'But . . .' I say.

'No more of your pathetic excuses,' she says. 'Please! Until you learn to treat Sooty better you can sleep in his kennel and he can have your bed.'

She turns and storms back inside.

I look at Sooty. This is all his fault.

I kneel down, hold his head and stare into his eyes.

'Are you happy now?' I say.

He wags his tail, leans forwards and licks my mouth.

I think I'm going to be sick.

BUT THAT'S MECHANICAL BIRDS FOR YOU. JUST A FUNNY, FUNNY LOT.

45

DID I TELL YOU ABOUT OUR LAST MECHO-BIRD CAMP? WOW!

A Crazy, BAD, Dumb, Bad, Bad, Dumb, CRAZY, BAD IDEA

I'm standing in the middle of the school oval.

I'm trembling.

And I'm covered in sweat.

Am I crazy to be doing this?

No.

In fact, I'd be crazy *not* to do it.

This sort of opportunity doesn't present itself every day. Besides, it's a perfect morning for flying. The sky is clear and it's not too windy.

Mr Pickett, Danny's dad, is running this year's school fete. It's on today. Danny and I have been here since 6 a.m. helping him set up. For the last hour we've been filling balloons with helium. We're going to put them along the school fence and front gates. We've also got some weather balloons that were donated by the local army disposals store. We've painted a letter on each one. Put them together and they spell 'FETE'. Mr Pickett's idea is to attach them to four really long pieces of rope and float them high above the school to let people know the fete is on. Which is what's going to happen. Eventually. But first I'm just going to take them for a little joy flight.

Danny and I have tied two enormous bunches of party balloons to the front straps of my backpack, and the four giant weather balloons to the back of it.

The balloons are tugging at my backpack, pulling me upwards. My toes are just touching the ground. The only thing keeping me from floating off is that Danny is holding on tightly to my arm and the rope around my waist.

'Okay,' I say to Danny. 'Let the rope out about ten metres and then haul me back in. Got that?'

'Are you really sure you want to do this?' he says. 'I don't think it's a good idea.'

'Are you kidding?' I say. 'Of course it's a

MR SCRIBBLE MEETS MR RUBBER.

ARGH!

IS THIS THE END FOR MR SCRIBBLE?

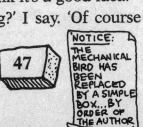

NOTICE: THE MECHANICAL BIRD HAS BEEN REPLACED BY A SIMPLE BOX...BY ORDER OF THE AUTHOR

good idea! It's a great idea! It's a brilliant idea! It's perfectly safe. Just don't let go of the rope.'

Danny shakes his head.

'I won't let go,' he says. 'You can count on me.'

I'm not leaving anything to chance, though. That's why I'm holding a long sharp stick. Just in case.

If Danny does let go, then all I'll have to do is burst a couple of balloons and I'll descend slowly and safely. It can't go wrong.

'Come on, Danny,' I say. 'Before your dad gets back. He said he'd only be half an hour. We don't have much time.'

'Are you ready?' says Danny.

'Roger,' I say.

'Roger?' says Danny, looking around. 'Who's Roger?'

SOMETIMES I AM STRUCK WITH THE THOUGHT THAT YOU ARE ALL JUST CRAZY!

'Nobody,' I sigh. 'It's what pilots say. It means yes.'

'Oh yeah,' says Danny. 'I forgot. I'm just a bit nervous. If Dad finds out about this he's going to kill us.'

'Come on, Dan,' I say. 'Your dad will never know. I'm just going straight up and straight down.'

Danny nods.

48

'All right, Roger,' he says. 'Have fun.'

He lets go of my arm.

My backpack pulls even harder against my chest and I quickly start floating upwards.

I can't believe it. It's working. I've always wanted to fly, and now I am.

I flap my arms and call down to Danny.

'Look at me!' I say. 'I'm flying!'

'Go, Roger!' yells Danny.

'Stop calling me Roger, you idiot!' I yell.

'Roger, Roger!' yells Danny.

I shake my head. I can't believe I'm trusting this moron with my life.

I look all around me. It's a great view. I can see forever. The neighbourhood is laid out below me like a little toy village. And there's my house! Wow!

I wish I could stay up here all day, but it's cold and the wind is much stronger this far up. I should have worn a jumper.

'Danny!' I yell. 'That's enough. Bring me down!'

He looks pretty small from up here, like a little boy flying a kite.

He waves back. Then he starts letting out the rope to make me go higher. He obviously can't hear me.

'No, Danny!' I scream. 'Not higher! Lower!' I point towards the ground.

He points at me and points back to the ground and shrugs.

I nod wildly.

'Yes, Danny!' I yell. 'Down!'

He starts trying to pull me in, but he seems to be having trouble. The wind is really strong up here, and I'm starting to drift towards the edge of the oval.

Danny is leaning back, straining on the rope. But it's no use. He's not pulling me down—I'm pulling him along.

Uh-oh.

This is not fun anymore. And the wind seems to be getting even stronger.

'Come on, Danny,' I call. 'You can do it!'

But he can't hear me. And he can't do it, either. He is being dragged to the edge of the oval where it slopes steeply away to the fence. He takes two giant steps, trips and tumbles down the bank . . .

I feel myself whoosh high and fast into the air. Danny has let go of the rope!

I can see him lying at the bottom of the bank, holding his leg. He's getting smaller and smaller and smaller.

50

Aaaaggghhh! I'm floating away!

What am I going to do?

How am I going to get down?

What if I just keep going up and up and up until I end up out in space?

This was a bad idea.

A dumb idea.

A crazy idea.

A bad, dumb, crazy idea.

A crazy, bad, dumb, bad, bad, dumb, crazy, bad idea.

And I've only got myself to blame. Which makes it even worse. I hate that.

Hang on. The stick! I forgot about my stick!

I don't have to worry about a thing. All I have to do is burst a couple of balloons and I'll go down instead of up. Mr Pickett won't be happy about me bursting the balloons, but at least I won't just disappear and never be seen again, which will make *me* happy.

I raise the stick as high above my head as I can. I try to poke a hole in the 'F' balloon but it just bobs away. The skin is tougher than I thought. I jab at the 'E' balloon. It bobs away as well. I try some of the party balloons but it's no use. There's nothing to push

FLOATING AWAY...

A PAGE NUMBER BOX.

ONE DAY ON THE HIGH VOLTAGE POWER LINES.

against. This stick was another bad, dumb, crazy idea.

I poke a few more times, but my neck's getting really sore from looking up at the balloons. I give up and turn around.

Oh no.

In front of me is the scariest thing I've ever seen.

High-voltage power lines.

There must be at least fifty of them—stretching in front of me like a gigantic horizontal spider web.

And I'm heading straight towards them.

If I don't do something fast I'm going to hit the lines and fry like a mozzie in a mozzie zapper.

I have to get rid of some of these balloons.

I can't pop them but maybe I can untie them.

I pull at the knots tying the party balloons to my pack, but I can't get them undone. They're too tight. It'll take me ages to get them untied. Time I don't have.

Maybe I should just take the pack off and let myself fall to the ground. But that would kill me. But so will the wires.

What to do? Fry or splatter? Splatter or fry?

BOX: A RIGID CONTAINER HAVING 4 SIDES, A BOTTOM AND A TOP.

Actually, I'd rather die of old age.

My only hope of that, though, is to go *over* the power lines. But how? How do I get myself up higher?

I know! I could jettison some stuff. The more I can get rid of, the higher I'll go.

I'll start with this stupid stick. It was no help at all.

I drop it. It falls through the air like a spear. Lucky there's nothing but grass and trees underneath me.

What else can I get rid of?

I look at my runners. The soles alone must weigh at least two kilograms. They're brand-new but they're going to have to go.

I raise my feet up, untie the laces and pull off the runners. My socks as well. They go sailing downwards.

But I'm still not high enough. I need to get rid of more.

I untie the rope from around my waist and let it go. I search through the pockets of my jeans and pull out everything I've got. A used Band-Aid. A half-eaten Jaffa. A chewing gum wrapper. A dead cockroach—at least I think it's dead. My wallet. It's got ten dollars in it. I saved it to spend at the fete. But I have

OTHER PICTURES OF LISA.

to let it go. It kills me to drop all this stuff, but it will really kill me to keep it.

I rummage deep in my shirt pockets. I pull out a photograph of Lisa Mackney. No, not that. Anything but that. I cut it out of our school magazine. It's not a very good picture, because it only catches her side-on. Well, more like the back of her head—most of which is covered by the back of somebody else's head—but I know it's her. And it's all I have. I can't throw it away.

I look at the power lines.

I've made a lot of progress. A lot of very good progress. I'm a fair bit higher than I was. But still not high enough. I need to lose something else. But I haven't got anything else. Except my pants that is.

I watch as my jeans drop away towards the ground.

I hate to see them go. They're my favourite pair. And it's freezing up here. If I don't fry on the wires I'll probably die of exposure.

The wires are getting closer but unless I get a bit higher I'm not going to clear them.

I look at Lisa's photograph in my hand. I'm going to have to let her go.

54 BOTTOM

It flutters and spirals away. It's the saddest thing I've ever seen in my life.

But also the most fantastic.

Because it's saved my life.

Lisa Mackney has saved my life!

I lift my legs, curl my toes and clear the power lines with less than a centimetre to spare. I hear the deadly hum of the electricity as I skim over the top. If this hadn't been such a crazy, bad, dumb, bad, bad, dumb, crazy, bad idea in the first place, I would be very proud of myself.

I take a few deep breaths and try to relax. But not for long. Because now I've got a new problem. Well, an old problem actually but it's getting worse. I've got goosebumps all over my legs and my toes are turning purple. And I'm still no closer to the ground. How am I going to get down and get back to the school before Mr Pickett does?

I'M GOT HUMAN BUMPS ALL OVER MY LEGS.

I'm going to have to try to untie the party balloons again.

I work away at the knots. It's hard because not only are they tied on very tightly, but my fingers are almost numb with cold.

YOU GOOSE!

Finally, I loosen the knots and untie the balloons from the shoulder strap of my pack.

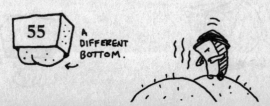

55

A DIFFERENT BOTTOM.

BACKYARD OPERA.

1. MIAOW LIKE A CAT TO GET NEXT DOOR'S DOG BARKING.

2. BANG TWO METAL BIN LIDS TOGETHER TO GET THE DOG ON THE OTHER SIDE HOWLING.

3. ROLL A METAL BIN DOWN THE FOOT PATH.

4. CHECK THE DOGS ARE ALL BARKING.

5. CALL THE POLICE AND ASK THEM TO COME ROUND... HOPE THEY USE THE SIREN.

There must be at least two hundred of them. They fly into the sky above me like it's five minutes before the siren on Grand Final day at the MCG.

I begin to drop quite quickly. They were giving me more lift than I realised. For a moment I'm worried that I'm going to keep dropping and not stop, but I level out just a bit above the tree-tops. That's better. Not perfect, but a lot better. It beats hovering above high-altitude high-voltage lines any day.

I'm floating slowly over the roofs of houses. I can see into all the backyards. A dog is going nuts. Barking and jumping up at me. It sets off other dogs and soon there's a chorus of barking and howling.

Some kids are pointing and waving at me. I wave back. They run out of their yard and onto the street and begin following me. They are joined by others and within minutes there's a small crowd of people following me. Not just kids, either. There are a few adults as well. One of them is pointing a video camera at me. Probably hoping I'll have an accident so he can flog it to one of those funniest home video shows.

'Don't just watch me!' I yell. 'Help me!'

56 BOX.

'What do you want us to do?' yells a woman.

Now that's a very good question.

I don't exactly know.

They don't teach you how to deal with situations like this in school. That's the trouble with school. They don't teach you anything useful. There should be a subject called 'What to do if you find yourself floating about twenty metres off the ground with no pants on and four large weather balloons attached to your backpack'. Or, even better, they could deal with this and many other situations by lumping them together under one subject called 'Crazy, bad, dumb, bad, bad, dumb, crazy, bad ideas'. Now *that* would be useful.

A BUSY DAY AT THE MODEL CHICKEN LEG CLUB.

I'm heading towards a long row of pine trees. I can hear buzzing and whining. Oh no, not more power lines! No, it's louder than that.

MAKE FUN OF CHICKEN LEGS WILL YOU!

As I float over the top of the pine trees I see lots of people. They are all looking up, as if they've been waiting for me to appear. But it's not me they're looking at.

Gulp.

The air is filled with model aeroplanes. They are looping and diving around each other.

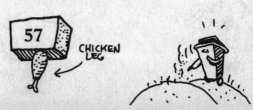

57

CHICKEN LEG

A CLOSE SHAVE AT THE MODEL PLANE CLUB.

I suddenly realise what this is.

It's the local model aeroplane club. They're putting on a display at the school fete today. They must be practising.

People are pointing and laughing at me.

'Look out!' I yell. 'I'm coming through!'

But there's too much noise. And the men flying the planes are too busy twiddling the knobs on their remote control units to even notice me.

I float right into the middle of the action. The planes are swooping and diving and whining around me like a pack of killer mosquitoes. But I can't swat them. They're much too big for that, and their propellers look much too sharp.

I hear a particularly loud whine behind me.

I turn my head and see a large biplane with orange wings.

I KNOW WHO YOU ARE AND WHERE YOU LIVE...

...ONE WHO LAUGHS AT CHICKEN LEGS.

Uh-oh. I'm in trouble.

Or am I?

This could be just what I need to get me away from here and back to the school. I might even beat Danny's dad.

I watch as the plane flies closer and closer. I flex my fingers and wait for my chance. I'm only going to get one shot at this.

58

WHEEL

As it passes me I shoot my hand out and grab onto its tail.

It starts pulling me away at high speed. I can feel the wind from the propeller on my face.

I carefully turn the plane towards the right. I fly around in a wide semicircle and head back towards the school.

I hear yelling.

'Hey, you little thief! Let go of my plane!' calls a man in a red cap.

'I'm not stealing it,' I yell. 'I'm just borrowing it. I'll bring it back. I promise!'

But he obviously doesn't believe me. He is furiously working away at his controls and I feel the plane start to turn back again.

'Oh no you don't,' I say. I reach over and pull the aerial out of the cockpit of the plane. I'm in control now.

I turn the plane towards the school and travel back the way I came. Over the houses, over the yards. It's the same as before except now I'm travelling ten times faster and this time I go *under* the power lines instead of over them.

I can see the school oval ahead of me. There are a few more people there now than

ONE DAY AT THE REMOTE CONTROLLED CAT CLUB.

HORSE HEAD.

when I left. They're unpacking cars and setting up tables. The jumping castle is being inflated. Imagine one of them filled with helium. Now that is a good idea. You could float *really* high.

There's Danny, at the edge of the oval. He's still sitting on the ground, holding his leg. He's looking up, talking to somebody. Who is that?

Oh no.

It's Mr Pickett!

Rats. I didn't beat him. I'm going to cop it after all.

They look up and see me.

Danny gets to his feet and waves.

I point the plane downwards and head towards the cricket pitch. It will make a great landing strip.

When I'm a few metres from the pitch I straighten the plane up and level out.

'Grab me!' I yell.

Mr Pickett starts running. He wraps his arms around my legs and pulls me to the ground.

Danny limps over and takes the plane out of my hand. He flicks the throttle switch off.

'That was so cool!' he says. 'You're amazing!'

60

'Shut up!' growls Mr Pickett. He keeps hold of me while he takes the pack off my back. 'What on earth did you think you were doing?' he yells. 'Of all the irresponsible, fool-hardy stunts to pull!'

'It's not his fault, Dad,' says Danny. 'I shouldn't have let go of the rope.'

'That's beside the point!' yells Mr Pickett. 'He should never have been up there in the first place!'

Danny looks at me and shrugs. It was a good try and I appreciate it, but Mr Pickett is on a roll.

'You could have been killed!' he says and points at the sky. 'These balloons were sup-posed to be used to advertise the fete. They should have been up there by now. Instead I come back and find that you've taken them for a joy flight. An insanely dangerous one, I might add!'

I look over Mr Pickett's shoulder.

The small crowd that was following me through the streets is coming through the gates of the school. But it's not a small crowd anymore. It's huge!

There are kids, adults, dogs, cars, police, an angry-looking man in a red cap and even

a television news van with a satellite dish on the roof. A cameraman is hanging out the window with his camera pointed at us. They must be transmitting live footage back to their newsroom.

Wow! I'm going to be on TV. I'm famous. That's great, but I wish I had some pants on.

Mr Pickett pauses. He's so mad he can't think of what to say next.

A little kid comes up behind him and tugs on his jumper.

He wheels around and looks down.

'What do you want?' he growls.

'How much for a ride on the balloons?' says the kid, pointing to my pack, which Mr Pickett is still holding.

'What?!' he says.

He looks up and notices the crowd. There are people everywhere. Already there's a long queue at the sausage sizzle and the drinks stall. Chasing me through the streets has obviously made everyone pretty hungry and thirsty.

Business is booming. Mr Pickett can't be mad at me now. I wish I could say the same for the man in the red cap, though. He snatches his plane off Danny and walks up to me.

62

'I want a word with you,' he says.

'Smile!' calls a newspaper photographer.

The man turns. He smiles for the camera. Mr Pickett puts his arm around my shoulder and smiles too.

'Remind me to murder you later,' he grunts.

I grin.

Looking at the crowd I've gathered I can't help thinking that my balloon flight wasn't such a bad idea after all.

In fact it was a good idea.

A great idea.

A brilliant idea.

A good, great, brilliant, great, great, brilliant, good, great idea.

Rubbish

It's Tuesday night.

A very important night.

And not just because it's Valentine's Day, either.

It's rubbish-bin night.

And what's so important about rubbish-bin night?

Well, according to my mum and dad, the health of the entire neighbourhood depends on me remembering to put the rubbish-bin out.

Because if I forget to put the bin out, the garbage men can't empty the bin.

And if the garbage men can't empty the bin then we can't fit any more rubbish into it.

And if we can't fit any more rubbish into

the bin then the rubbish will spill out over the top and onto the ground.

And if there's rubbish on the ground then the rats will come, and if the rats come, people will get sick, disease and pestilence will spread throughout the neighbourhood and everyone will die.

And, the worst thing is that I will get the blame.

That's why rubbish-bin night is the most important night of the week: the fate of the neighbourhood is in my hands. Every man, woman and child is counting on me to remember to put the bin out.

And I haven't failed them yet.

I never forget.

Each week I tie a piece of white string around the little finger on my left hand to remind me.

The trouble is tonight I've tied it a bit too tightly and it's making my little finger throb. It's so tight that I can't get the knot undone. I'm going to have to cut it with a pair of scissors.

I go downstairs to the kitchen.

I pass Dad in the lounge room.

'Have you remembered what night this is?' he says.

65

'Yes, Dad,' I say.

'Have you put the bin out yet?'

'Not yet,' I say.

'Well, don't forget,' he says. 'I don't want rubbish spilling out all over the ground. It will attract rats and . . .'

'I know, Dad,' I sigh. 'If the rats come people will get sick, disease and pestilence will spread throughout the neighbourhood and everyone will die.'

'You think it's all a bit of a joke, do you?' he says, leaning forward in his chair and pointing his finger at me. 'Well, we'll see how much of a joke it is when we're up to our ankles in rubbish and rats and you've got bubonic plague and you've got boils all over your body, funny-boy! And we'll all have a good laugh when bits of your lungs come flying out of your mouth and . . .'

'Okay, Dad!' I say. 'I get the picture! I'm going to put the bin out, all right?'

'Now?' he says.

'In a minute,' I say. 'Right after I cut this string off my finger.'

'Don't forget,' he says.

'I won't, Dad,' I say. 'I promise.'

I swear my dad's getting crazier by the day.

66

I go into the kitchen, pull open the second drawer down and start rummaging for the scissors.

Mum comes into the room.

'Have you put the bin out?' she says.

'Not yet, Mum,' I say. 'I'm just about to.'

'Well, don't forget,' she says. 'We don't want . . .'

REASONS WHY YOU SHOULD NOT RUMMAGE IN DRAWERS THAT CONTAIN SCISSORS.

'Rats,' I say.

'How did you know I was going to say that?' she says.

'A lucky guess,' I say.

The phone rings.

I go to pick it up.

'Don't touch that!' says Jen, pushing past me and beating me to the phone. 'That'll be Craig. Besides, shouldn't you be putting the bin out? It stinks—I can smell it from my room.'

'I'm surprised you can smell anything above your own stink,' I say. Jen makes a face and picks up the phone.

I just keep standing there. She hates it when I listen in on her calls.

Jen puts her hand over the mouthpiece.

'Mum,' she says, 'Andy's listening to my call.'

'I am not!' I say. 'How can I be listening if you haven't even started talking?'

67

'You're *going* to listen,' she says.

'Pardon?' I say.

'I said "you're *going* to listen",' says Jen in a louder voice.

'What?' I say. 'I can't hear you. I think I've gone deaf.'

'Mum!' says Jen.

'Andy,' sighs Mum, 'you've got a job to do. Just go and do it.'

'All right,' I say, but I don't move. I just keep standing near the phone.

'Andy,' says Jen.

'Okay, okay!' I say. 'I'm going!'

'That's not what I'm talking about,' she says, holding the receiver towards me. 'It's for you.'

'For me?' I say.

'Yes,' says Jen. 'Hard to believe, isn't it, but apparently someone wants to talk to you.'

'Who?' I say. 'Who is it?'

'Whom shall I say is calling?' Jen says into the phone.

She smirks.

'It's Lisa Mackney,' she says.

'Lisa Mackney?' I say. 'Are you sure?'

'Do you want me to ask her if she's sure she's Lisa Mackney?' she says.

'No!' I say, grabbing the receiver.

68

Lisa Mackney! Wow! She must have got my Valentine's card. I slipped it into her bag this morning. I wonder how she guessed it was from me. Maybe the perfume on the envelope gave me away. Well, it wasn't exactly perfume. I couldn't find any, so I sprayed it with the pine-scented air freshener we use in the toilet.  It went all over my clothes and I stunk of it all day. I guess she must have noticed.

Jen is still standing beside the phone.

'Mum!' I say. 'Jen's listening to my call!'

'As if I'd want to listen to one of your juvenile phone calls,' she says, walking out of the room. 'I've *got* a life.'

'Hello?' I say.

'Hi, Andy—it's Lisa,' she says.

'Oh, um, er . . .' I stutter, trying to think of something clever to say. 'Hi!'

'I hope you don't mind me calling you,' she says.

Is she kidding? It's only the best thing that has ever happened in the history of the world. But I can't say this. She might think I'm making fun of her. I have to act cool.

'No,' I say.

I can't think of anything else to say. Which is funny because I've got so much to

DYE YOUR
HAIR
GREEN.

BUY AN
INFLATABLE
MUSCLE
SHIRT.

PAY GIRLS TO
HANG AROUND
YOU.

GET YOUR MUM
TO CALL UP
EVERYONE
AND TELL
THEM.

say. I want to tell her how beautiful she is and how much I love her and how I wish she would be my girlfriend . . . but I can't find the words.

'You're not busy, are you?' she says. 'I can call back later if you'd like.'

What do I say to this?

If I say I'm not busy, she might think I'm some sort of loser with nothing better to do than just sit around the house. But if I say I am busy putting the bin out, she might think that I'm some sort of loser with nothing better to do than put the bin out.

I know honesty is supposed to be the best policy but in this case I think that dishonesty is even better.

'No, I'm just taking a breather,' I say. 'I've been doing a bit of weight-training . . . those five hundred kilogram weights can be pretty tough.'

'You do weight-training?' she says.

'Oh, a little,' I say.

'A little?' she says. 'Five hundred kilograms is a lot!'

'Oh not really,' I say. 'That's just a warm-up. It's the thousand kilogram weights that are really hard.'

70

I hear Lisa gasp.

So far, so good. I think she's suitably impressed.

'Andy,' she says, 'can you be serious for a moment?'

'Huh?' I say. 'I was being serious!'

Dishonest, but serious.

'I need to talk to you,' she says. 'It's important. I need to ask you a question. A serious question.'

'Okay,' I say. 'What is it?'

'Did you send me the card?'

'What card?' I say, playing dumb.

'The Valentine's card,' she says.

'Oh, that card,' I say, as casually as I can. 'Yes, I did.'

'I thought so!' she says.

There's an uncomfortable silence. I'm not sure what to say next.

'I wanted to thank you,' she says.

'That's okay,' I say.

'No, I meant in person,' she says. 'I was wondering if we could meet tomorrow morning? Before school?'

I can't believe it! She's practically asking me out on a date!

'Andy?' she says. 'Are you there?'

No, I'm not here. I'm somewhere between the Earth and the moon I'm so happy. I have to try to come back. I have to answer her.

'Yes!' I say. 'I'm here. Where would you like to meet?'

'How about outside the park near the school?' she says. 'About 8.30?'

'Okay, Lisa,' I say. I'm keen to get off the phone now before I say anything stupid. 'See you then.'

'See you,' she says. 'And, Andy?'

'Yes?' I say.

'It wasn't a joke, was it?'

'What?' I say.

'The card?'

'No!' I say.

'Good,' she says. 'I'm really looking forward to it.'

'Me too,' I say. I want to add, 'because you're beautiful and I love you', but I can't actually make the words because my mouth is just opening and closing like a fish's.

I hang up.

I can't believe it.

The most beautiful girl in the world just rang up and asked me out on a date. What if she asks me to go out with her? Can she do

72

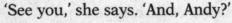

that? Can a girl ask a boy? I don't see why
not. What if she asks me to marry her? Can
we do that? Are we old enough? Will I need a
ring? Or does the one who asks have to give
the ring? What if she asks me to kiss her? I've
never kissed a girl before. Not really. Not on
the lips. How do you do that? I'd better go
and practise on my mirror.

THE KISS.

I don't walk back up the stairs. I float.

Lisa rang me.

Lisa rang me and asked me out.

She asked me out.

I have to keep repeating it so that I can
believe it.

Lisa rang me.

She asked me out.

I didn't ring her. She rang me. She must
really like me after all. After everything bad
that's happened.

I float into my room and flop onto my bed.

She loves me.

She loves me.

I lie on my bed and think about tomorrow
morning.

I can see it now.

I'm walking up the road to the park. I
have a dozen roses in my arms.

73

Lisa is standing there, looking beautiful.

Everything around her is sort of blurry, like in one of those romantic photos they have in the front of photographers' shops, but she is in the middle in perfect focus.

She smiles and waves.

'Hi, Lisa,' I say, in a deep, strong and confident voice.

She looks into my eyes.

I look into hers. I feel like I'm melting.

'Hi,' she says in a voice so soft and beautiful that she sounds like an angel.

I give her the roses.

'These are for you,' I say.

She looks at the roses. Her eyes fill with tears.

HER EYES
FILL WITH
TEARS

'They're beautiful,' she sobs. 'Just beautiful . . .'

FROM PG.129
FURTHER
DETAILS
OF DR
WONKLE'S
DREAM
DE-NEBULIZER
HAVE BEEN
MOVED TO
PAGE: 90

'Not as beautiful as you,' I say, putting my arms around her.

I bury my face in her soft perfumed hair—every strand shining like it's spun from the finest gossamer.

'Oh, Andy,' she says, 'you are so thoughtful . . . so wonderful . . . so gentlemanly . . .'

'You forgot handsome,' I say.

'And handsome,' she says.

74

YUM!
SPLUNCH.
CHOMP.

'And manly,' I say.

'And manly,' she says.

'And strong,' I say.

'Be serious,' she says.

'I was being serious,' I say.

She stares at me.

FUNNY JOKE FOR PEOPLE WHO UNDERSTAND EGYPTIAN HIEROGLYPHICS.

'Before we go any further I have to ask you a question,' she says.

'Anything,' I say. 'Ask me anything you want.'

'Promise me you will answer truthfully, my darling,' says Lisa.

'I promise,' I say.

She leans forward and whispers into my ear.

Her breath sends shivers through my body that run right down into my toes. I feel dizzy and I hear a roaring sound as the blood rushes to my head. It's so loud I can hardly hear what she's saying. All I can hear is a roaring sort of grinding sound.

Lisa pulls away from me.

She's studying my face.

'Well?' she says.

'Well what?' I say.

'What's your answer?'

'What was the question?' I say.

HMMM RUBBISH

'I said,' she says, raising her voice above the roar, 'did you remember to put the bin out?'

'The what out?' I say.

'The bin!' she screams.

The bin? The bin? What bin?

Oh no—the bin!!!

Suddenly the sun goes behind a cloud and the street around us is alive with rats—Lisa's hair turns to cobwebs, the skin peels off her face and she crumbles into a crumpled mummy-like heap on the footpath. I scream. The whole street dissolves—Lisa disappears. I open my eyes. The room's full of light. How could that be? I look across at the clock. It's 7.30 a.m. I must have fallen asleep! The room is full of the roar and grind of the rubbish truck out in the street. And my finger is throbbing. I forgot to cut the string off. But even worse—I forgot to put the bin out!

I jump off the bed and charge out of the room. Luckily I'm wearing my Action Man pyjamas. I can run faster when I'm wearing them. I leap down the stairs in one huge bound and sprint for the back door.

I grab the bin. It's heavy—feels like it weighs at least a thousand kilograms—but luckily it's a wheelie bin. I tip it backwards and

run as fast as I can with it down the drive—just in time to see the rubbish truck turn the corner at the bottom of the hill and disappear.

Aaggh!

Dad's going to kill me!

Mum's going to kill me!

If they don't die from the bubonic plague first, that is.

I have to get this bin emptied . . . and there's only one way to do it.

The rubbish truck can't be that far away. They have to stop all the time. And I'm a very fast runner when I need to be.

I take off down the hill.

Or rather the wheelie bin takes off down the hill and drags me along with it. If it wasn't for the stink this would be quite a fun ride. But at the bottom of the hill the ground levels out and I have to start pushing. I turn left up the next hill.

I can't do it!

It's too hard.

The bin is too heavy.

The hill is too steep.

Then I remember the rats.

I think of all the people in the neighbourhood who are going to die because I forgot to empty the bin. Little innocent children—still sleeping—oblivious of their fate. Oblivious of the fact that they are going to be deprived of life because I can't even remember a simple thing like putting the bin out on rubbish night. The fate of the neighbourhood depends on me. I have to go faster.

I bend over and put every bit of strength I have into pushing the bin up the hill. I'm going up at such an angle that the lid of the bin flips back and whacks me on the head. It's a blow that would have knocked anyone else out, but not me. I've got a very hard head. I flip the lid back and keep pushing. Nothing can stop me.

The roaring of the rubbish truck is louder now. I'm getting closer. I crest over the top of the hill and see it less than a hundred metres away.

'Stop!' I yell. 'Stop! You forgot one!'

There are two men in fluorescent yellow vests running alongside the truck. They pick up the last two bins in the street and put them on the tray at the back. It lifts the bins up and empties the rubbish into the top of the truck.

I'm pushing the bin down the hill as fast as I can.

The men put the empty bins onto the side of the road and jump back onto the truck to ride to the next street.

'No!' I yell. 'Please stop!'

One of them sees me coming and calls out to the driver.

The truck stops and I run up to it with my bin.

'Well, if it isn't Action Man!' says one of the men.

'You forgot this one,' I say, panting hard. 'From the next street.'

'Forgot it?' he says. 'That's not possible. Are you sure it was on the street when we went past?'

'Yes,' I lie. This is another one of those situations where dishonesty is the best policy. It's a lie that could save many lives.

He looks at the other guy.

'Did you forget this one?'

'Nope,' says the other one. 'I would have seen it.'

'Sorry, Action Man,' says the first guy. 'If it had been there we would have got it.'

'Are you saying you don't believe me?' I say.

'I'm not saying anything, mate,' he says.

'I'm just saying we can't take it. If it's not outside the house then we're not permitted to empty it. For all I know you could be from out of our area—you could be trying to dump your rubbish illegally.'

'But I'm not!' I say. 'Why would I want to do that?'

'You'd be surprised what people try,' he says, thumping the side of the truck. 'Okay, Mac!'

The truck takes off again and the man jumps up on the back.

I watch helplessly as the truck turns into the next street.

But I don't give up that easily.

I know a short cut through to the next street.

All I have to do is take the bin through, put it into position and hide. They'll empty it just like a regular bin.

I run down the hill a bit further and then turn right into a laneway. I push the bin for all I'm worth and within seconds I'm there.

Up in the distance I can see the yellow flashing lights of the truck. They've only just turned into the street. They're still too far away to see me.

Good.

I push the bin across the opening of the lane and head towards the nature strip, but the bin hits the gutter and lurches sideways.

I lose control and it hits the ground, spilling rubbish everywhere.

I can't believe what I'm seeing.

Half of the stuff from our garage is lying on the road. Mum and Dad must have had another cleanout. I hate it when they do that. They've thrown out some really good stuff. And some of it's mine. My old floaties. A house I made out of matchsticks. And my electric racing car set! I know the controls are missing, pieces of the track are broken and the cars have lost all their wheels, but that's no reason to throw out a perfectly good electric racing car set!

I'd better check there's nothing else of mine in there. I stand the bin up and look inside.

Oh no. I don't believe it!

She's chucked away the most valuable thing I own in the world—my faithful bath and shower companion—my rubber duck! I can see its little yellow beak peeking out from under the rubbish.

LIFTED BY
A SWARM OF
HOUSEFLIES,
RUBBISH
DUCKIE
ROSE UP
INTO THE SKY.

I look up.

The rubbish truck is about halfway along the street. I've got just enough time to get my duck and then scram.

'Don't worry!' I say. 'I'll save you!'

I lean down into the bin, but I can't reach. It's right at the bottom.

I have to lean over further.

Uh-oh.

Too far!

I fall into the bin, headfirst into something squishy and smelly. It doesn't taste too good, either.

And what's worse, I can't move.

I can't get up.

The roaring of the truck is getting louder.

I kick my legs to try to make the bin fall over so I can wriggle out.

But my kicking is useless.

All it does is make the lid of the bin fall shut on top of me.

Now I'm trapped.

And nobody knows I'm in here!

The truck is right beside me. I can hear it. I feel the bin roll off the nature strip and land on the road with a bump. I think it's being put on the tray. I'm rising into the air. It's just

like being in an elevator except much smellier.

I'm yelling my head off but it's no use. They can't hear me above the noise of the truck.

I clutch my duck. The bin tips upside down and we are dumped into the back of the truck with all the other rubbish.

The stink!

The stench!

The horror!

This has got to be the most disgusting thing that's ever happened to me.

I'm being churned around with all the rubbish. I try to scream but I get a mouthful of used tissues. Everything is a blur as bin after bin of fresh rotting rubbish is dumped on top of me. Mouldy vegetables, putrid fish and disposable nappies . . . I come face to face with a dead cat, but only for a moment—the churning just won't stop. Every time I catch my breath and work my way to the top of the pile a new bin-load knocks me down and the churning continues.

I've got to get out of here!

I've saved the neighbourhood, but I'm going to die!

ALSO FOUND IN ANDY'S RUBBISH TRUCK.

STEPHANIE FROM DOWN THE ROAD.

MR SMITH'S FALSE LEG.

STATUE OF LIBERTY.

MR SMITH'S THREE REAL LEGS.

83

THE SYMPTOMS OF BUBONIC PLAGUE.

YOUR FEET SWELL UP AND TURN INTO CATS.

WHEN EVER YOU SNEEZE YOUR HANDS DROP OFF.

YOUR HEAD BECOMES LOOSE.

MEE OWW

YOUR MOTHER PUTS YOU OUT ON GARBAGE NIGHT.

WAK!

I'll get bubonic plague.

I think I can feel it coming on already.

Dad's right.

There is nothing funny about being up to your knees in rubbish—and when it's over your head it's even unfunnier.

What a pity I won't live to tell him that.

Because I can't fight it anymore.

I'm going to die, suffocated in rubbish.

I press my rubber duck to my chest, close my eyes and prepare for the end.

That's weird.

Everything has gone quiet.

The churning has stopped.

Maybe there's still hope.

I dig my way up out of the rubbish towards the light.

I push my head through a load of mouldy bread, empty dog food cans and used kitty litter.

But I don't care. I can see the sky!

I raise my duck above my head.

'We're going to make it,' I say.

My duck quacks with joy.

I squirm and wriggle the rest of my body out from under the rubbish until I'm sitting on top of it all.

HMMM RUBBISH.

I wipe the slime from my eyes and look around.

We're travelling along a main road. The truck is obviously full and they're heading back to the tip to empty it. I've got to get out before that happens. I don't want to spend the rest of my life as landfill.

We pull up at a set of traffic lights.

This is my chance to escape.

I climb down over the back of the truck onto the platform, and just as the truck starts moving again, I jump clear. I hit the ground running, trip and roll into the gutter.

Ouch.

It hurts, but it's better than being in a rubbish truck any day.

'Are you all right?' says a voice.

A beautiful voice.

The voice of an angel.

I must be dead.

The bubonic plague got me after all and I've gone to Heaven.

But there's something familiar about that voice.

I open my eyes.

It's Lisa.

Lisa Mackney looking down at me.

'Andy?' she says.

'Lisa?' I say. 'When did you die?'

'Die?' she says. 'What are you talking about? We arranged to meet, remember?'

I sit up.

I look around.

This is not Heaven. This is Hell.

I'm outside the park.

Right where I said I would meet Lisa.

I'm right on time, but everything else is wrong. As wrong as it possibly could be.

There she is looking clean and fresh and princess-like, her soft hair shining in the morning sun. And here am I, sitting in the gutter in my pyjamas covered in rubbish, surrounded by flies, clutching my rubber duck.

'I should have known you weren't serious,' she says, pinching her nose and backing away from me. 'I should have known it was all a joke.'

'No, it wasn't!' I say, getting up and stepping towards her. A big slimy chunk of maggot-infested meat slides off my shoulder and plops onto the ground in front of her.

She puts her hand over her mouth and takes another step back.

'Keep away from me!' she says. 'You . . . you . . . you stink!'

I step towards her—kitty litter, cigarette butts and broken eggshells fall from my clothes and hair as I move.

She turns and runs.

I watch her. The girl I love. Running away from me in disgust.

What was supposed to be the best morning of my life has turned out to be the worst.

And the worst thing about it is that she's never going to want to kiss me now. All that practice on the mirror for nothing.

But at least I got the rubbish out. At least the neighbourhood is safe once more from the bubonic plague.

There's no telling how many lives I've saved.

Not to mention my rubber duck.

Perhaps all is not lost, after all.

I'm going to go home, cut this stupid string off my finger and have a long shower. A really long shower. I might even use some more of that air freshener—it was pretty strong. Then I'll go to school and explain everything to Lisa.

I'm sure she'll understand. In fact, I can see it now.

When she hears about what I've done, she'll realise what a hero I am. She'll apologise for saying that I stink. She'll beg me to forgive her. I will, of course. And then we'll kiss.

It's lucky I did all that practice on the mirror, after all.

ANYONE WISHING TO PURCHASE ADVERTISING RIGHTS TO THIS SPACE PLEASE CONTACT: www. andygriffiths. com.au

Um-mah!

'**B**ut, Mum,' I say. 'I can't look after them. I'm busy.'

'Busy?' says Mum. 'Busy doing what? Watching television?'

'It's a very important programme,' I say. 'We have to watch it for school.'

Mum comes into the room.

I quickly change the channel.

'I saw that!' she says. 'Since when did cartoons become important programmes?'

'Ever since they were first invented,' I say. 'But fine. If you don't want me to do my homework then I won't. I'll fail. I'll drop out. I'll become a full-time babysitter.'

'Oh come on,' says Mum. 'It's just for half an hour. They won't give you any trouble.'

I groan.

'Are you kidding?' I say. 'They're psychos!'

'Don't be ridiculous,' says Mum. 'Look at them. They're lovely little girls.'

She points towards the kitchen. The girls are sitting at the table having a tea party with their dolls.

'Yeah, they're lovely when you're around,' I say, 'but it's just an act. As soon as you leave the room they go crazy.'

Mum rolls her eyes and picks up her car keys.

FROM PG. 74.

DR WOMKLE SAYS "MY DREAM DE-NEBULIZER REALLY WORKS". FOR A FREE HOME TRIAL SEE Pg. 151

'That's enough, Andy,' she says. 'I'm not *asking* you—I'm *telling* you. You're looking after them and that's that.'

The girls—my cousins—have been here for three days now and I'm almost out of my mind. They have been messing up and breaking stuff all over the house and I've been getting the blame. Mum is looking after them while my aunty is in hospital having a baby. I wish she'd hurry up and have it. The sooner these kids are out of this house the better.

'Don't leave me here with them, Mum,' I say. 'Please, I beg you . . .'

'Bye-bye,' she calls to the girls, ignoring

me. 'I'm going out for a while but Andy will look after you, won't you, Andy?'

She fixes me with an icy glare. I know what that look means. It means that I'd better take very good care of the girls . . . or else.

'Bye-bye,' call the girls. They wave and smile so sweetly that for a moment I almost believe they are completely innocent normal little girls.

Mum leaves.

I go to the lounge room window and watch her back the car out of the driveway and drive away down the hill.

I look at the girls.

They're still having their tea party.

So far, so good. Maybe this won't be so bad after all.

I sit back down in front of the TV and change the channel back to my cartoon. Luckily I haven't missed too much. The mouse is still chasing the cat around, hitting him on the head with an enormous hammer. That poor cat. He never wins. He always gets clobbered. Uh-oh. Now the mouse has a box of matches. He sets the cat's tail on fire.

Wow. That's so realistic I can practically smell the smoke.

Wait on.

I *can* smell smoke.

That's not coming from the TV. It's coming from the kitchen. And what's that racket? There's all this banging and clattering. I don't think the girls are playing tea party anymore.

I jump up and run to the kitchen.

There's a haze of blue smoke and the smell of burning rubber.

Jemima's standing up on a chair next to the bench with a fork in her hand which she's about to stick into the top of the toaster.

'NO!' I say.

She turns around.

'But it's stuck,' she says, completely unaware of how close she is to being electrocuted. 'It's burning.'

'Just leave it,' I say, moving towards her. 'I'll do it.'

'I can do it myself,' she says.

'NO!' I scream.

But it's too late. She plunges the fork into the toaster.

I stop. I can't touch her. She must have 240 volts flowing through her body. The electricity might go from her to me.

But I can't just leave her there.

Maybe if I put rubber dishwashing gloves on . . .

'Got it!' says Jemima, turning to me with something black and smoking on the end of her fork. It doesn't look like toast—it's a dishwashing sponge.

RUBBER DISHWASHING GLOVES AS A FASHION ACCESSORY.

AT WEDDINGS.

'See,' she says. 'I told you I could do it myself.'

'But . . . how . . . what . . .' I stutter, 'why didn't you get electrocuted?'

AT PARTIES.

'Because I turned the switch off and pulled out the plug first, you dum-dum,' she says. 'Everybody knows to do that.'

'And what were you doing burning a sponge anyway?' I say.

GRADUATIONS.

'It's not a sponge,' she says, talking to me like I'm stupid. 'It's toast for my tea party.'

'It's not toast,' I say. 'It's a sponge and it smells disgusting!'

Something clatters to the floor behind me.

I turn around.

FUNERALS.

Eve has her dolls lined up against the wall and is throwing knives at them.

'And what do you think you're doing?' I say.

'I'm playing circus,' she says.

'Well, cut it out,' I say. 'You're not allowed to do that!'

'Who says?' says Eve.

'I say!'

'You're not the boss of us,' she says, throwing another knife at her doll. The knife misses the doll and takes a chunk of plaster out of the wall.

'Yeah, you can't tell us what to do,' says Jemima, throwing the fork she was using on the toaster at me.

I duck. The fork flies over my head.

'Right,' I say. 'You're in big trouble!'

The girls giggle and run out of the kitchen. I run after them but they're gone. I can't see them anywhere. I walk through the lounge room to the foot of the stairs.

CRASH!

A chess and Ludo set lands at the bottom of the staircase. Chess pieces and Ludo tokens go flying all over the floor.

I look up.

A game of Monopoly crashes down on my head. Houses and hotels go everywhere. Monopoly money flutters down around me.

Jemima and Eve are hanging off the banister. They're smiling and looking very pleased with themselves.

'Get down here and pick this all up!' I yell.

They just laugh.

'Now!' I say.

I start to climb up the stairs.

MR SCRIBBLE CLIMBS THE STAIRS.

Jemima pulls a picture off the wall and frisbees it at me.

I reach out and grab it as it flies through the air. It's a photo of me when I was a little boy. I look like such a nice little kid—not an out-of-control brat—not like them.

I put the picture down and start up the stairs again. But Jemima opens the door of a display case hanging on the wall. Mum keeps her crystal animal collection in there.

'No, Jemima!' I say. 'Don't touch that! They're Mum's!'

Too late.

She flings a small sparkly object at me.

I catch it. It's a little crystal mouse. Mum treasures those stupid animals. If anything happens to them I'll be in big trouble. Even bigger trouble than if anything happened to the girls.

Eve grabs one as well and throws it.

I catch it in my other hand.

'No more,' I plead. 'No more! I've got no hands left!'

Jemima smiles and then lobs a third one.

NOT YOU!

I watch as it arcs through the air towards me.

This is the greatest challenge of my life. But I have to do it.

I position myself underneath it, tilt my head back and open my mouth as wide as I can.

The little crystal animal drops onto my tongue. Safe and sound. All that practice throwing bits of food up into the air and catching them in my mouth at the dinner table has finally paid off.

The girls stand at the top of the stairs and giggle.

'I'm going to kill you!' I scream, although with my mouth full it sounds more like 'WYMEGWANAILLOO'.

I spit the crystal animal out of my mouth and put it and the other two in my pocket.

I look up towards Eve and Jemima but they're gone. No doubt to find something else to throw.

I run up the stairs.

I look in my room.

They're not there.

I check Jen's room.

They're not there either.

YOU!

96

I look in Mum and Dad's room and the bathroom but there's no sign of them.

Where can they be?

I check under all the beds, in all the wardrobes and behind all the curtains.

They're gone.

Vanished.

'Eve! Jemima!' I yell. 'Where are you?'

'Here!' they call.

That's weird.

Sounds like they're outside.

But they couldn't be outside.

Could they?

Yes, they could!

I look at the window.

I feel sick.

I can see a row of tiny fingertips lined up neatly along the windowsill.

They're hanging outside the house!

Hanging from the first floor!

I rush across to the window. I look down at them.

'You can't catch us,' sings Eve. 'You can't catch us.'

'Girls,' I say, 'this is not a joke. You could kill yourselves.'

'Don't get your knickers in a knot,' says

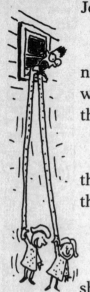

Jemima. 'We're just hanging out the window.'

'You're just about to die!' I say.

I brace my legs against the wall underneath the window, reach out and grab Eve's wrist with one hand and Jemima's wrist with the other.

Got them!

Now all I have to do is pull them in. But they're heavier than they look. As I try to lift them up it's hard to keep my feet on the floor.

'You're hurting my arm!' says Jemima.

'Shut up!' I say. 'I'm trying to save you.'

'Um-mah!' says Eve. 'You told Jemima to shut up.'

'You shut up too!' I tell her.

'Um-mah,' they both say.

I struggle some more, but it's hopeless. I'm not pulling them in—they're pulling me out!

I can't do it.

I'm bent over double, already half out the window and I can feel my knees scraping against the window ledge.

In a few moments we're all going to fall!

Not that the girls seem to care.

They're giggling and kicking their feet as they dangle in the air.

I hear a clanging noise.

98

What's that?

'Hey, there's a pipe here,' says Jemima.

She's right.

Her feet are almost touching a drain pipe that runs along the outside of the house. It juts out a fair way from the wall. If I can just lower them onto it then I can leave them there while I go and get the ladder.

'Can you stand on it?' I say.

'Sure,' she says.

I lower Eve onto the pipe as well.

'Now I'm going to let go,' I say. 'I want you to stand on the pipe and lean into the wall. Stay there until I get the ladder! Don't move.'

Jemima starts bobbing and tapping her foot on the pipe.

'DON'T MOVE!' I yell.

'You're a bossy boots,' says Eve.

I sigh.

'Please don't move,' I say. 'It's for your own good.'

That's the trouble with babysitting little kids. If they hurt themselves it's the babysitter who gets the blame. It's not fair. Babysitting sucks.

I pull myself back into the window. I've got to be quick. If they fall I'm going to be in

more trouble than I've ever been in in my whole life.

I sprint downstairs and through the kitchen. It's a big mess. Knives all over the floor.

I slip on one and go skating across the room headfirst into the fridge.

Ouch.

I pick myself up and stagger outside.

I check the side of the house.

But the girls are not there.

I'm too late.

I feel sick.

PLAYING WITH KNIVES CAN BE DANGEROUS.

I look down at the ground under my window, expecting the worst.

But they're not there either.

CRASH!

A roofing tile shatters on the ground beside me.

I look up.

Eve and Jemima are standing on the roof.

'What the hell are you doing up there?' I say.

'Um-mah,' says Eve. 'You said a rude word. You'll get in trouble.'

PLAYING WITH FLUFFY RABBITS CAN BE DANGEROUS.

'Not as much trouble as you're already in!' I say. 'I told you to stay put until I got the ladder!'

HEY, I ASKED FIRST.

'We thought you weren't coming,' says Jemima. 'So we climbed up the pipe.'

Eve bends down, picks up a roofing tile and throws it at me.

I step back. It shatters at my feet.

'Hey!' I say. 'Cut it out!'

'You can't stop us!' says Jemima. 'You're not the boss.'

'We'll see about that,' I say.

I run to the garage. The ladder is stuck behind a stack of folding chairs and old paint tins. I move them all out of the way and carry it outside.

I lean the ladder up against the house and climb up onto the roof.

The girls are gone.

But that's impossible.

'Eve?' I call. 'Jemima? Where are you?'

I walk up the roof to the highest point.

I can't see them.

How could they not be here?

Unless they climbed back down the pipe.

Those girls are unstoppable.

I walk back down the roof and get onto the ladder.

I'm climbing back down when I hear giggling.

101

I look down.

The girls are standing at the bottom of the ladder.

Uh-oh.

'Now, Eve!' yells Jemima.

They both pull the ladder out from the side of the house so it's standing straight up in the air.

'No!' I yell as the ladder tips backwards and I go crashing into the garden.

DR HAMISH McFLOGGIT'S BRILLIANT INVENTION, THE HALF LADDER.

I hear the girls laughing hysterically. I push the ladder off and struggle to my feet, just in time to see Eve running down the driveway.

'Eve!' I yell.

She looks up at me, laughs and keeps running.

I run after her but she's already rounding the corner at the bottom of the hill.

I have to catch her. There's a busy inter-section at the bottom of that hill. It's really dangerous. And I should know. I nearly got killed going through it in a pram once.

I see Jemima's pink bicycle lying on the lawn.

I don't really like the idea of riding a tiny pink girl's bike down the hill, but it's my only hope.

I pick up the bike, jump on it and start pedalling as hard as I can. My knees are practically hitting my chin. I feel like an idiot.

'Nice bike, mate!' yells a kid from the side of the road. 'Pink really suits ya!'

This is embarrassing. My face is burning. I just hope Lisa Mackney doesn't see me.

Despite how awkward the bike is to ride I'm gaining on Eve. I draw level and then swing the bike around in front of her and skid to a stop.

'Gotcha!' I say, grabbing her arm.

But she pushes me away with her other hand. I lose my balance on the bike and fall over.

She runs back up the hill.

I pick myself and the bike up, and limp back up the hill, dragging the bike behind me.

I get back to the house. I'm completely puffed, my leg hurts and Eve is nowhere to be seen.

I open the front door and walk in.

I can hear screaming.

It's coming from the lounge room.

I can't believe what I'm seeing.

Jemima is hanging onto the overhead fan and swinging around.

I've got to hand it to her. Even I've never thought of doing that.

ONE FINE DAY AT THE ELDERLY CITIZENS CLUB.

Beside her there is a stack of furniture—a stool on top of a chair on top of the glass-topped coffee table—and on top of the swaying stack is Eve. She's poised, her arms outstretched, trying to grab onto the fan as well.

'Don't do it!' I yell, diving towards her. 'You'll break it!'

Too late.

Eve jumps. She misses the fan and ends up holding onto Jemima's waist.

I go crashing into the stack of furniture. It collapses around me. The chair falls onto the coffee table and smashes the glass.

Jemima is swinging around on the fan, with Eve hanging off her.

'Wheee!' screams Eve. 'This is fun!'

I run underneath them to try and pull Eve off. I grab her legs, but she won't let go.

There's a cracking noise.

Eve screams.

Jemima screams.

I scream and watch in horror as the fan is wrenched from the ceiling.

WELL! WHO ARE YOU?

104

ME?

The girls come crashing down on top of me.

Without thinking, I put my arms around them and roll us all out of the way.

The fan crashes down onto the carpet, right where we were just lying. The lounge room is covered in white dust and rubble.

These girls are really out of control.

I've got to stop them before they wreck the whole house.

But how?

They won't listen to me. They only behave in front of adults.

That's it!

I have to disguise myself as an adult.

And I've got just the thing.

'If you don't stop misbehaving right now I'm going to go and tell Mr Paddywhack!' I yell.

'Who's that?' they say in unison.

'He's a very scary man!' I say. 'And he hates naughty children. He's going to make you behave yourselves!'

'He sounds stupid,' says Jemima.

'All right,' I say. 'That does it! I'm going to get Mr Paddywhack right now!'

Mr Paddywhack is this crazy character I

made up for a school concert last term. I dressed up in a white lab coat, a wig made out of the top of an old mop, a yellow hard hat and a diving mask, and I held a tennis racquet in each hand. It was funny because all the little kids were really scared of me—they thought I was going to whack them with my racquets. That's how I came up with the name.

I go up to my room. My costume is still sitting at the bottom of my wardrobe.

I put on the lab coat, the mop wig, the yellow hard hat and the diving mask.

I get two tennis racquets from the hall cupboard. I'm not really going to hit them of course. I'm just going to give them a fright.

I come barrelling down the stairs like a madman waving the racquets above my head.

WHY ARE THERE NEVER MECHANICAL BIRDS IN STORIES LIKE THESE?

Jemima and Eve are jumping on the couch.

'I SMELL TWO NAUGHTY CHILDREN!' I yell. 'AND I'M GOING TO WHACK THEM!'

'No you're not,' says Jemima, studying my face closely.

'OH YES I AM!' I yell.

'No you're not,' says Jemima. 'You're not even real. You're just Andy dressed up in a stupid wig and hat.'

...THE MECHANICAL BIRD.

'I'M MR PADDYWHACK!' I bellow.

'Where's Andy then?' says Jemima.

'He's . . . he's . . .' I say. I didn't expect this question.

'You don't know where he is,' says Jemima, 'because *you're* Andy!'

Jemima jumps from the couch and grabs the racquets out of my hand. I try to get them back but she's too fast. She hands one to Eve.

'Whack him!' she says.

Eve whacks me in the leg with the bat.

'Ouch!' I yell.

Jemima whacks me on the bum.

'Take that, Mr Paddywhack!' she squeals.

Eve whacks me on the foot with the edge of the racquet.

I'm getting out of here. I can't take anymore.

I start running.

They chase me.

I run out of the lounge room, into the kitchen and down the hall. But I can't shake them. They're hot on my heels. I run back into the lounge room, through the kitchen and out into the hall again. I run around and around, trying to get away from them. They're maniacs.

COUCH WARS.

COUCH WE NEED YOU, THE WORLD IS UNDER ATTACK!!

COUCH CLIMBS TO THE TOP OF THE HIGHEST MOUNTAIN

STOP ALL THIS...

BUT BEFORE HE COULD SAVE THE WORLD...

HE WAS STOLEN BY TWO COUCH THIEVES.

I run so fast that I almost lap them. It's hard to tell who's chasing who.

'COME HERE!' I roar.

The girls look over their shoulders, startled to see me so close. They squeal. I lean forward and snatch the racquets off them.

Fantastic! For the first time today something has gone my way!

'NOW I'VE GOT YOU,' I yell, as we run down the hallway. 'PREPARE FOR A WHACKING!'

'Andy! What on earth do you think you're doing?'

Mum is standing in front of us.

When did she get home? I didn't hear her come in.

'Help!' screams Jemima.

'Help!' screams Eve.

They run to Mum and hug her legs.

'Save us!' screams Jemima. 'Andy's gone crazy!'

'I haven't gone crazy,' I say. 'They have!'

'What do you mean by dressing up and scaring the girls like this?' says Mum, her arms around them, trying to comfort them. 'I ask you to look after them and I come home and find you chasing them and threatening to hit them with tennis racquets!'

'*They* were chasing *me*!' I say.

SORRY, PAL...

I can see Mum looking around the lounge room, taking in the destruction. The stool and the chair lying on top of the broken coffee table, the wrecked fan, and the chunks of ceiling all over the floor.

'I suppose you're going to tell me all this is the girls' fault as well?' says Mum.

'Yes!' I say. 'It is. I tried to stop them. In fact I saved their lives.'

Mum snorts.

'Don't make it worse by lying,' she says. She strokes the girls' heads. 'Are you all right? You poor darlings. What happened?'

'We were just trying to have our tea party,' says Jemima, sniffling, 'and he came into the kitchen and started bossing us around.'

'He wouldn't let me play with my dolls,' says Eve.

'But,' I say. 'She was . . .'

'Then he held us out of his bedroom window,' says Jemima. 'And he hurt my arm.'

'And he said rude words,' says Eve.

'But,' I say. 'They were . . .'

'He left us on the roof!' says Jemima.

'Not exactly,' I say. 'I was . . .'

'He swung on the fan and broke it!' says Jemima.

THE DEATH OF A CEILING FAN.

THE END.

BUT, I'M THE MECHANICAL BIRD.

109

'And he broke the table too,' says Eve.

'No, I didn't,' I say.

'You did!' says Jemina. 'It was your fault.'

'Well, it was sort of my fault,' I say, 'but . . .'

'Then he dressed up as that scary man and chased us round the house,' sobs Jemima.

'And he tried to hit us with tennis racquets,' wails Eve.

THIS STORY IS NEARLY OVER. THE NEXT ONE IS SURE TO BE ABOUT MECHANICAL BIRDS.

Gee. I've got to hand it to them. Those girls are the best truth-twisters in the world. They're pretty good at fake crying too. They're even starting to make *me* feel sorry for them.

They're standing there with their sweet innocent faces and big tear-stained eyes. I don't stand a chance. There is nothing I can say. No way is Mum going to believe the real truth.

I HOPE IT'S ABOUT LONE CHICKEN LEGS.

Poor Mum. I feel sorry for her too.

I think the full extent of the damage is beginning to dawn on her. She's just staring into the lounge room, shaking her head.

'Andy, how could you?' she says. 'The place is a mess. Everything is wrecked!'

I wish there was something I could say. Something I could do that would make her feel better.

HERE'S MY CONTRACT.

110

BUT!

Hang on! There is!

'No, Mum,' I say. 'Not *everything*!'

'Well, it certainly looks that way to me,' she says.

'But I saved these,' I say. 'Your crystal animals. Look.'

I put the tennis racquets down and reach into my pocket.

That's funny.

I thought I put three in there but it feels like a lot more.

I hold out my hand.

'Um-mah,' says Jemima.

'Um-mah,' says Eve.

'Well?' says Mum, bending down to pick up one of the tennis racquets. 'What have you got to say for yourself?'

I look down at the shattered crystal in my hand.

'Um-mah,' I say.

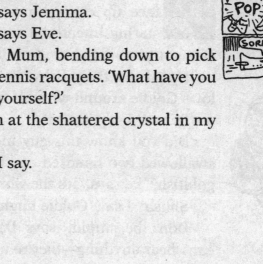

Pinch

anny is in my bedroom, pressing his face up against my goldfish bowl, staring intently at my new goldfish. He's got his hand above Goldie's bowl.

'Here fishy, fishy, fishy,' he says, as he follows Goldie around with his fingers.

'Danny,' I say. 'Quit it.'

'Did you know this guy in Texas in 1970 swallowed two hundred and twenty-five live goldfish?' he says. 'It's the world record.'

'Shush!' I say. 'Goldie might hear you!'

'Don't be stupid,' says Danny. 'Goldfish can't hear anything—they're underwater.'

'It doesn't matter whether they can hear you or not,' I say. 'Goldfish are very sensitive. They pick up on your vibes. Especially Goldie.'

'What do you think it would be like to have a live goldfish in your stomach?' says Danny. 'Do you think you'd be able to feel it swimming around and around inside you?'

'I'm warning you, Danny,' I say.

But he's not listening.

He dips his hand into the bowl and grabs Goldie. He tips his head back and dangles her above his mouth.

'That's not funny!' I yell. 'Put her back!'

Danny just laughs.

He lowers Goldie until she's almost touching his lips.

He's going to do it. He's really going to do it. I've got to stop him.

I throw myself across the room, but I'm too late.

Danny drops Goldie into his mouth and swallows her. In one gulp. Whole.

'Hey!' I say, pushing him in the chest. 'You ate my goldfish!'

'It was an accident,' he says. 'It slipped.'

'That's a lie and you know it!' I say. 'You deliberately ate her!'

'Shush,' says Danny. He tilts his head as if listening to a faraway sound.

'Hey,' he giggles, 'I *can* feel it! It tickles.'

I'm so angry I'm shaking. Not only has he swallowed Goldie, he doesn't even care. Well, I'll make him care.

I clench my fist tight and swing at his head, but he steps nimbly to the side and I end up punching the air.

I look at my fist. I look at Danny. He is bouncing around on his tiptoes like a boxer.

'Missed me,' he says. 'Have another go!'

I punch again, but Danny skips out of the way.

'Too slow,' he says.

I line him up again.

Then I let fly. And this time I connect.

KAPOW!

Danny's head snaps back.

IT WAS A LUCKY PUNCH!

There's an enormous cracking sound and the next thing I know Danny's head is flying across my room towards the window.

It bounces off the glass and splashes down into my fishbowl. His head completely fills the bowl. His distorted face looks out at me, his mouth slowly opening and closing.

This is crazy. It can't be happening. Punching someone can't make their head come off, can it? And even if it could, shouldn't they be dead? Their headless body shouldn't be

114

staggering around bumping into walls should it?

Because that's what Danny's headless body is doing.

And what's that noise?

It sounds like laughter. But it's horrible laughter. Evil and high-pitched. And it's coming from inside Danny's body.

This is too crazy. I mean, his head coming off was crazy, but this is TOO crazy.

I'm getting out of here.

I try to run but I can't lift my feet off the ground. They feel like they're nailed to the floor.

I bend down and try to lift them up with my hands, but they won't budge. The high-pitched laughter is getting louder and louder and louder . . .

Oh no . . . I don't believe what I'm seeing . . . Hundreds of mini-Dannys are pouring out of the neck of Danny's headless body.

Wave after wave after wave.

Hundreds of them.

Thousands.

They're pouring out of his neck, down his arms and leaping to the ground . . . and, worst of all, they're heading towards me. Laughing their tiny heads off.

TAKE THAT! 115

They're really close to me now. They swarm around my feet and start climbing onto my runners.

'Hey!' I say, shaking my foot. 'Get off!'

But they don't stop.

They keep leaping. I shake even harder. They fly off and land on the carpet, but immediately regroup and keep trying to climb onto my shoes. It's like standing on an ants' nest. They're getting crazier and crazier. And there are more coming. They keep streaming out of Danny's neck. They're everywhere.

I've got no choice.

I'm not normally a violent person, but I'm going to have to squash them.

I start stomping.

But it doesn't stop them.

As I flatten them they split into two and each mini-Danny becomes two even minier-Dannys. And the minier-Dannys laugh even harder and louder than the mini-Dannys.

They all start leaping onto the bottom of my jeans. They're climbing up my legs like spiders. I've got to stop them. If I don't they'll be all over me in seconds.

I look around.

There's a can of flyspray on the windowsill.

I brought it into my room to use against mosquitoes—I hope it works against mini-Dannys.

I snap the lid off and start spraying my legs.

As the spray hits them the mini-Dannys fall backwards onto the floor, spin around on their backs and kick their legs in the air.

But it doesn't stop the others from trying.

For every one that I kill, two take its place. And when I kill those two, four more jump on, laughing the whole time. The noise is incredible.

This is so horrible. It can't be happening.

Hang on.

Maybe it's not happening.

Maybe it's just another one of my crazy dreams. I've been having a lot lately.

If it's a dream then all I have to do is pinch myself and I'll wake up and everything will be fine.

I put the flyspray down on the windowsill and pinch the skin on my forearm. Ouch.

I blink.

The light hurts.

I look around.

I'm in my bed, drenched in sweat.

117

GIANT
DANNY

ANDY

At least I hope it's sweat.

What a relief!

It *was* just a dream.

A nightmare.

But at least I'm awake now.

I look over at my fishbowl.

That's strange.

Goldie's missing.

But I only dreamed that Danny swallowed Goldie . . . didn't I? If Goldie's really gone, that means I wasn't dreaming and if I wasn't dreaming that means that . . . well, I'm not sure what it means . . .

And why is the room shaking?

Is this an earthquake?

The plaster on the roof above my bed is cracking. A big chunk of it falls onto my bed.

IT'S
GIGANTIC
DANNY!!

I hear a loud splintering sound. Dust and bits of plaster rain down onto my bed and the room is filled with light.

It's like the roof has been lifted off the house.

Maybe it's not an earthquake. Maybe it's a cyclone.

No!

It's a gigantic Danny!

A Danny that towers into the sky.

118   OH,
YEAH!

A Danny that looks as big to me as I must have looked to the mini-Dannys.

He's hideous.

He's horrible.

But he's unmistakably Danny.

He tosses the roof away as if it's no heavier than the lid of a shoebox. It crashes to the ground. The whole house shakes.

Danny throws back his head and laughs. An enormous ear-splitting laugh that seems to fill the whole world.

He reaches down, picks me up by the collar of my pyjama top and lifts me high into the air. He tilts his head back and holds me above his mouth.

Oh no!

He's going to eat me—just like he ate Goldie!

It is a horrible view from up here.

I can see every filling in his mouth. His big disgusting tongue. I can see every crack and fissure—and there's this yellow gunk all over it. But the worst thing is his breath. It smells like dead fish. And it's blowing all over me.

I don't want to go in there.

I don't want to die.

But there's nothing I can do.

I'm dangling in the air.

And then Danny lets go.

I'm going down, down, down.

Down into the slimy dark-redness of Danny's throat.

It's all around me.

The warm squishy walls.

Pressing.

Squishing.

Digesting.

Digesting!

I've got to get out of here.

I've got to go up.

But I'm going down.

Suddenly the squishing stops.

I fall into a big red cave.

Dark.

Dripping.

Wet.

I land on something squelchy. Everything's sort of wobbly and unsteady. It's like being in a jumping castle that's covered in slime.

I guess this must be Danny's stomach.

What am I saying? I can't be in Danny's stomach.

This can't be real.

I must be dreaming.

That's it. Of course. I'm still in my dream.

Or am I? Is it a dream, or maybe it's some sort of weird hallucination. What if I've gone mad but I don't know I've gone mad because not knowing I've gone mad is part of the madness? But then the fact that I'm thinking this means that I *must* know I'm mad so I *can't* be mad. But how can I be sure that I'm not just dreaming that I'm mad—or that I'm mad and I'm just having a regular dream? I could try pinching myself again, but that didn't really help the first time. That's how I ended up in here. What if I pinch myself and I end up in an even worse dream? I couldn't stand it. This is bad enough.

No.

I'm just going to have to deal with the situation as it is. It's the only way.

I have to find a way out of Danny's stomach. But how?

As my eyes adjust to the dimness I can see a whole landscape emerge from the gloom around me.

It has a sort of lunar feel—everything is covered in some kind of white powder. It's all over me. I brush myself down and sniff my

fingers. I know that smell. It's sherbet! Judging by how much of it is down here, Danny must live on the stuff.

There's a big lake in front of me. I have to be careful. That could be Danny's stomach juices. I crouch down for a closer look. It doesn't look like stomach juices though. It's sparkling and full of bubbles, like lemonade. I put my finger in and taste a bit. It *is* lemonade!

AND DEEP IN THE CAVERNS OF HIS STOMACH I MET OLD BEN BUNN, A CASTAWAY. HE TOLD ME MANY STORIES OF HIS YEARS LOST IN DANNY'S STOMACH.

On the other side of the lemonade lake there appears to be a snow-capped mountain range. It's not like a normal mountain range though—it's pink and white and brown. As I peer closely I can see that it's actually ice-cream. And next to it there looks like hundreds—possibly thousands—of donuts. All sitting around in huge piles like stacks of old tyres at a car wreckers.

No wonder Danny is acting so strangely.

He lives on a diet of pure sugar.

Except for the occasional human, that is.

But how am I going to get out?

I look up. There's no way I can climb back up the walls of Danny's throat. They're too slippery. Besides, the opening I fell through must be more than a hundred metres above me. I couldn't reach it even if I tried.

HA HA MISSED!

AND THAT!

I look all around me.

I see something flashing in the lemonade lake. Something that glitters.

I move towards it.

It's Goldie!

I reach down and pick her up.

'Don't worry, Goldie,' I say, slipping her into my pyjama pocket. 'I'll get us out of here!'

I hear a long low noise in the distance.

It sounds like a foghorn.

I look up. In front of me I can see a tunnel sloping downwards.

SUDDENLY, IT ROSE BEFORE ME. FOUL AND AWESOME !! THE BODY OF A HUGE CHICKEN LEG AND THE EYE OF A MAN, JUST AS BEN BUNN HAD DESCRIBED IT.

That could be a way out.

I start running as fast as I can, but as I run further along the tunnel it gets darker, the smell gets worse and the foghorn gets louder.

Uh-oh.

If that's the only way out, then I'd rather stay in.

I run back the way I came.

Perhaps being in Danny's stomach is not so bad after all. At least there's ice-cream. And donuts. And sherbet. And all that lemonade. No wonder Danny burps so much.

Actually, that gives me an idea.

When you mix sherbet and ice-cream and

lemonade together it bubbles and froths. If I stirred all this stuff up together in Danny's stomach maybe I could create enough gas to make him burp it—and me—up and out of here.

It's worth a try.

I scrape the sherbet into a big pile and push it into the lemonade. The lake starts frothing and bubbling.

Good, but no sign of a burp yet.

I grab enormous handfuls of ice-cream and add them to the lake.

AS I CLUNG DESPERATELY TO MY PIECE OF TOAST, THE WARNINGS OF BEN BUNN RANG IN MY EARS: 'BEWARE THE GIANT SQUID!!!'

Better—the froth is building—but still I need more.

I scrape more sherbet and hurl more ice-cream.

Eventually the froth starts to overflow the lake. The whole spitting, popping, bubbling mess is out of control. It's all around me.

Suddenly the stomach is filled with a low rumbling noise. The spongy floor wobbles like jelly. I put my arms out and try to stop myself from falling, but I trip and stumble backwards.

I lose my balance, but I don't fall. Instead, I'm swept up in a tornado of burp gas and sucked back up the way I came.

MISSED.

124

I shoot up the throat at an amazing speed.

I'm going so fast that I miss the turn-off to Danny's mouth and go hurtling up into his nose.

This is very bad.

If I come flying out at this speed I could be killed.

But hang on!

I'm flying headfirst into a forest of nostril hairs.

I grab one. Some nostril hair! It's as thick as a piece of rope.

I swing up, hit the wall of Danny's nose and swing back again. This is even more fun than swinging on the clothesline. I swing back and forth a few times before slowing down and stopping.

Okay, I've avoided death by splattering. Now to get out of Danny's nose safely.

But just as I'm about to let go of the nostril hair, I see a new danger.

Danny's finger!

He's picking his nose!

I climb the nostril hair as far up as I can to try and get out of the giant finger's way, but it's no use. The finger is filling the entire nostril. It's like an enormous battering ram.

125

It's pushing me up against these big rubbery beanbags.

Except they're not beanbags.

And they're not made of rubber.

Erggh. That's disgusting! I'd rather die any other way than this.

I'm being pushed deeper and deeper into them. It's getting hard to breathe.

Suddenly I'm being rocketed forward again—attached to the end of Danny's finger.

I blink as I emerge into the light.

Danny points his finger towards his eyes and studies the end of it. He sees me.

He starts to laugh.

The overpowering stench of his breath makes me almost lose consciousness.

What's he going to do with me?

He's got to let me go now.

Surely he's made me suffer enough.

He moves his finger towards his mouth.

Oh no.

That's disgusting.

I don't mind admitting that I've picked my nose occasionally—well, more than occasionally, practically every day if you want to know the truth—but I've never, ever eaten it. Not on purpose, anyhow. I have my standards.

THE NOSE-PICKER'S GUIDE TO GOURMET FOODS OF THE HUMAN BODY.

SNOT: 4 STAR

EARWAX: STRONG TASTE, BUT RICH IN CALORIES.

BELLY BUTTON LINT: NOT RECOMMENDED.

TOE JAM: A TASTE THAT TAKES SOME GETTING USED TO, BUT WELL WORTH IT.

This is it. I've had all I can take.

I'm going to pinch myself.

Maybe things could get worse. But then again, it's hard to imagine anything worse than being covered in snot and eaten by a giant.

I pinch my arm as hard as I can.

I wake up in my bed.

I check the ceiling.

It's completely intact.

I check the floor.

No mini-Dannys.

So far so good.

Everything appears to be normal.

I check the goldfish bowl to see if Goldie is there. I can see something swimming in it. I suppose that's Goldie but I can't tell exactly. My vision is all blurry. And my eyes are burning.

I focus as hard as I can but what I'm seeing doesn't make sense.

It's not Goldie . . . it's . . . it's . . . it's me!

A tiny me swimming around and around the bowl.

But that can't be me . . . because I'm here . . . at least I think I'm here . . .

I look down at my body.

GANGS OF ANGRY YOUNG VACUUMS WILL OFTEN ATTACK LONE AND DEFENCELESS CLEANING LADIES.

← MR ANGRY BROOM.

THIS KIND OF BEHAVIOUR MUST NOT BE SIMPLY BRUSHED UNDER THE CARPET.

But I'm not me.

I'm a giant goldfish.

Wait! I'm obviously still dreaming . . . I've got to pinch myself again . . . but how do I pinch myself without arms or fingers? All I've got is a couple of useless fins!

I start flipping and flopping and flapping.

Crash!

I fall off the bed onto the floor.

There is a knock on the door.

'Help!' I yell. 'Help!'

But nothing comes out.

I can't talk. I can only open and close my mouth.

There is another knock.

'Andy?' says Mum. 'Are you awake yet?'

That's a very good question. I wish I knew.

The door opens.

Mum walks in.

'Why are you lying on the floor, you silly boy?' she says.

Boy? She called me a boy. That must mean that . . . I look down at my body. I'm not a goldfish anymore. Thank goodness.

'You have a visitor,' says Mum.

'Who?' I say.

'Danny,' she says.

MISSED ME.

128

@$*!

'No!' I yell. 'Not Danny! Keep him away from me!'

But it's too late—he's already in.

I can see his nostrils flaring.

I can see his fingers.

I know where they've been.

'Hi, Andy,' he says.

I scream.

'What on earth is the matter with you?' says Mum.

'Matter?' I say. 'I'll tell you what's the matter! He ate Goldie . . . then his head came off and a whole army of mini-Dannys attacked me and then he became a giant and ripped the roof off the house and ate me and then picked me out of his nose and tried to eat me again . . .'

Mum and Danny are laughing.

'Sounds like you've been having a bad dream,' says Mum. 'But you're awake now.'

'But am I?' I say. 'How can I be sure? Every time I think I'm awake the dream starts up again!'

'I had one of those once,' says Danny. 'I kept dreaming I was eating donuts. Millions and millions and millions of them. And every time I woke up I'd just be eating more donuts . . . it was really cool.'

IF YOU SUFFER FROM BAD NIGHTMARES YOU MIGHT LIKE TO TRY:

DR WOMKLE'S DREAM DE-NEBULIZER.

FOR FURTHER DETAILS SEE Pg. 74.

I'M NOT JUST CRAZY!

I'M VERY CRAZY!!

I scream again.

Mum sits on the side of my bed and strokes my head.

'Calm down, Andy,' she says. 'You're really awake now.'

'I am?' I say.

'Yes,' she says. 'There's nothing to worry about.'

But I'm not so sure. Something doesn't feel right.

I look at the goldfish bowl. Goldie's missing!

A bolt of fear shoots down my spine.

I point to the empty bowl.

'If I'm awake,' I say, 'then where's Goldie?'

Danny steps forward.

'There she is!' he says.

Goldie is flipping around on the carpet. Danny picks her up and puts her back in the bowl.

'There,' says Mum. 'See? Danny didn't hurt Goldie—he saved her. She must have jumped out of the bowl.'

But I'm still scared.

I don't trust Danny.

'I don't know, Mum,' I say. 'How do we know that he didn't already have her in his stomach and he just burped her up, put her

on the carpet and pretended to save her?'

Danny laughs.

'What are you on about?' he says.

'That's a very good question, Danny,' says Mum, getting up off my bed.

'Don't leave me, Mum!' I plead. 'Don't leave me alone with him!'

'Don't be ridiculous,' says Mum.

She leaves the room.

Maybe she's right.

Maybe I really am awake.

Maybe the dream really is over.

I look over at Danny.

My stomach drops.

HERE, HUMAN, HUMAN, HUMAN

He's pressing his face up against Goldie's bowl. He's got his hand above it and is following Goldie around with his fingers.

'Here fishy, fishy, fishy,' he says. 'Here fishy, fishy, fishy.'

HE HE

GOT!

Kittens, Puppies and Ponies

'm sitting in the gym listening to Mr Rowe drone on and on. Mr Rowe is the deputy head. He only gets to conduct whole school assemblies once or twice a year, and when he does, he makes the most of it.

'It's time some of you took a good long look at yourselves in a mirror,' says Mr Rowe. 'Ask yourselves if you like what you see. Listen to yourselves speak. Ask yourselves if you like what you hear. There are no such words as "gunna" and "youse" . . .'

I wish he'd hurry up and get to the most important bit. The announcement of the winner of the school short-story competition.

The reason I'm looking forward to this is

because the winner is going to be me.

How do I know?

It's simple.

Because I've written a story that is a sure-fire winner. The judges are going to love it.

I usually write stories full of action, explosions, monsters and guns. But I never win. The judges always go for the boring soppy stuff. So this year I've decided to give them exactly what they want. I've written the boringest, soppiest story in the world. Plus it has a happy ending. It can't fail.

DANNY THE DUNG BEETLE READS ABOUT HIS FAVOURITE CHARACTER: POOH BEAR.

Don't get me wrong.

I'm not proud of this story.

I just wrote it because it's the only way to win the competition. And the only reason I want to win the competition is to impress Lisa Mackney. She is always going on about books and writers and how she wants to be a famous author one day, so I figure the best way to get her to take me seriously is to win the competition.

DANNY THE DUNG BEETLE GETS HIT WITH A MALLET.

When Lisa sees me win the competition she's going to realise once and for all what a deeply thoughtful, poetic and sensitive person I really am.

Danny leans across.

'When am I going to get to read your story?' he whispers.

'I don't think it's really the sort of story you'd like, Dan,' I say.

'But that's not fair,' says Danny. 'I showed you mine. I won't laugh. I promise.'

'You really want to read it?' I say.

'Yes!' says Danny.

I pull a copy of my story out of my pocket and pass it to him.

Up until now I haven't shown it to anybody. I've kept it strictly top secret. I couldn't take the risk that somebody else might steal my idea and try to pass it off as their own.

Danny takes the story. I read it over his shoulder, just to make sure that it's as bad as I remember.

Kittens, puppies and ponies
by Andy Griffiths

SAM'S DRAWING OF KITTENS, PUPPIES + PONIES.

Once upon a time there was a magical kingdom called Lovelyville. Everything was lovely in Lovelyville. The people were lovely, the weather was lovely and the animals were lovely. There were no horrible spiders, poisonous snakes or giant cockroaches.

No. There were none of these things.

Just lovely animals like kittens, puppies and ponies. They played and frolicked and scampered around in the meadows causing no harm to anybody.

One day, one of the kittens had an idea.

'I know,' she said, 'let's go around to all the townspeople and give them each a big hug!'

'What a good idea!' said a pony. 'We could give them rides as well!'

'And lick their faces!' said a puppy.

'Yes!' said the kitten. 'Let's do it right now!'

And so all the animals set off.

The first house they came to belonged to Mr White.

JAZ's DRAWING OF LOVELYVILLE.

I'M SOOOO CUTE

135

MORE HUGS

I FEEL ASHAMED

I'M
CUTER
(I HAVE
BIGGER
EYES)

He opened the door and saw all the kittens and puppies and ponies of Lovelyville on his doorstep.

'Hello!' said the kitten. 'We've come to give you a big hug!'

Mr White looked at the playful, scampering group — their sleek well-groomed bodies shining in the morning sun — and his heart was gladdened. The kitten jumped up into his arms and hugged him. The puppy leaped up and licked his face. The pony came forward and Mr White climbed onto its back and went for a ride, tears of joy pouring down his face. And the animals didn't stop there. They kept going until they'd hugged and licked and given rides to every last person in Lovelyville.

'What a lovely day we've had!' said the kitten.

'Yes,' said the puppy. 'It's lovely to do lovely things for people.'

I'M MR WHITE,
AND I'M SO
CUTE YOU COULD
RUN ME OVER
WITH A ROAD
ROLLER.

SMOOCH

'Now Lovelyville is even lovelier than ever,' said the pony.

And the townspeople gave the kittens, puppies and ponies three cheers and everybody ate their vegetables, brushed their teeth and went to bed early.

The End.

Danny hands the story back to me. He's shaking his head.

'Well,' I say, 'what did you think?'

Danny takes a deep breath.

'You want the truth?' he says.

'Yes,' I say.

'It stinks,' says Danny. 'I hate it.'

'That's good,' I say. 'If you hate it then the judges will love it!'

'I wouldn't be so sure about that,' says Danny.

'You'll see I'm right,' I whisper. 'When I win.'

'No, that's where you're wrong,' says Danny. 'Because I'm going to win.'

'What?' I say. 'With a story about a giant mechanical chicken that goes rampaging

137

through the streets wrecking everything and killing everybody? You'll never win with that. The judges just don't go for all that action stuff.'

'How do you know what the judges like?' says Danny.

'Because I've worked it out,' I say. 'Every year we write stories about killer robots, killer aliens and killer chickens, right?'

'Yeah,' says Danny. 'So?'

'And have our stories ever won?' I say.

'No,' says Danny.

'Exactly,' I say. 'The winner is always Tanya Shepherd with some cute story about bunnies or teddy bears or elves. Well not this year, because I'm going to beat her at her own game.'

'Shush!' hisses a teacher standing at the end of our row.

Danny and I sit up in our chairs and look to the front.

But nothing has changed.

Mr Rowe is still going on and on and on. Blah blah blah. I wish he'd hurry up and finish.

I just want to get up there, collect my prize, make Lisa fall in love with me and get out of here.

Mr Rowe pauses, clears his throat, and

pauses again, as if he's forgotten what he's saying. He shuffles some sheets of paper and pulls out an envelope.

'And now for the winner of the short-story competition,' he says.

At last!

'We received a record number of stories for this year's competition—more than ten in fact—and the judges had a very difficult time deciding on a winner because they were all of such a high standard . . .'

That's funny. I would have thought mine was so obviously superior that it would have made the judge's job really easy. Perhaps he's talking about the runners-up.

'However,' says Mr Rowe, 'in spite of the difficulty, they have decided on a winner . . .'

Yes! Me, you gasbag! Just say my name and let me up there on that stage!

'. . . but before I announce the winner . . .'

Oh come on! Get on with it!

'I just want to say that as far as I'm concerned, every person who put an entry into the competition is a winner, and whether or not you actually win the competition is not important. The important thing is to have had a go . . .'

In case you're not familiar with Mr Rowe's speeches, what he's actually trying to say is that he's going to announce the winner (that's me) and that we're all going to pretend that the losers (that's everybody else) are winners as well. That's so they won't feel so bad about losing, which is quite pointless really because everybody will know that the losers are still the losers and that I, the winner, am still the winner.

'But without any further ado,' says Mr Rowe, opening the envelope and pulling out a small folded piece of paper, 'the runner-up of this year's short-story competition is . . . Daniel Pickett for his entry "Killer Mechanical Chickens From Outer Space".'

Huh? I don't believe it. Danny can't win second prize. Not with a story like that. The judges never award prizes to stories about robotic killers from outer space. Especially not if they're chickens. It doesn't make sense. Maybe they just felt sorry for him.

Everybody applauds. Danny stands up, walks to the stage, receives his certificate and walks back to his seat, his grin as wide as his face.

I lean across and shake his hand.

'Congratulations, Danny,' I say. 'You

missed out on the top prize but don't feel bad—you were up against me, after all.'

'Thanks, mate,' he says.

'And now,' says Mr Rowe, 'the moment you've all been waiting for . . . the winner of this year's short-story competition is . . .'

ME!

ANDY GRIFFITHS!

THE BEST!

THE STAR!

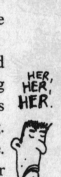

Mr Rowe pauses for dramatic effect and clears his throat.

'. . . Tanya Shepherd for her story, "The Ballerina Princess".'

I jump up out of my seat, my hands clasped above my head in victory and start heading towards the stage when I realise everybody is laughing. Except for Mr Rowe. He's frowning. I stop, halfway between my seat and the stage.

'Excuse me, young man,' he says. 'Is your name Tanya Shepherd?'

Everybody starts laughing again.

It takes me a little while to understand the question.

Tanya? My name's not Tanya. At least I don't think it is.

'Well?' says Mr Rowe.

I look at Mr Rowe standing there in front of me.

'No,' I say.

'Then sit down, you silly boy,' he says.

There's a fresh round of laughter as I turn around and walk back to my seat.

I can't believe what's happened.

Tanya Shepherd has blitzed me. Again.

She walks up onto the stage and Mr Rowe presents her with my certificate. It's all happening like a dream. No, not a dream. A nightmare. It's crazy, that's what it is. It's all wrong.

Danny leans across.

'Bad luck, mate,' he says, patting me on the arm. 'But don't feel too bad about it. Remember what Mr Rowe said? You're a winner too, not a loser. You had a go.'

I pull my arm away.

'That's crap and you know it!' I say.

'Yeah,' says Danny. 'I guess you're right. Your story really did suck. You *are* a loser.'

He's right.

I shouldn't have tried to write a story that the judges would like. I should have written a story that *I* would like.

In fact that's exactly what I'm going to do.

After assembly we go back to our classroom to get our lunches. Everybody goes outside except me.

I spend half of lunchtime rewriting my story.

I've finished the last sentence when Danny comes into the room.

'Okay, are you ready to hear it?' I say.

'Hear what?' says Danny.

'My story,' I say. 'I've rewritten it.'

'The one about the kittens?' he says. 'Why?'

'I've fixed it up.'

'Is there any hugging in it?' says Danny.

'No,' I say.

'What about face licking?' he says.

'No,' I say. 'I promise.'

'All right,' says Danny, sitting down. He doesn't look too happy.

I start reading.

Kittens, puppies and ponies: the TRUE story by Andy Griffiths

Once upon a time there was a magi-cal kingdom called Lovelyville.

Everything was lovely in Lovelyville. The people were lovely,
the weather was lovely and the
animals were lovely. There were
no horrible spiders, poisonous
snakes or giant cockroaches.

No. There were none of these
things.

Just lovely animals like kittens, puppies and ponies. They
played and frolicked and scampered around in the meadows
causing no harm to anybody.

One day, one of the kittens
had an idea.

'I know,' she said, 'let's go
around to all the townspeople
and give them each a big hug!'

'What a good idea!' said a
pony. 'We could give them rides
as well!'

'And lick their faces!' said
a puppy.

'Yes!' said the kitten. 'Let's
do it right now!'

And so all the animals set
off.

The first house they came to belonged to Mr White.

He opened the door and saw all the kittens, puppies and ponies of Lovelyville on his doorstep.

JAZ's DRAWING OF PULVERIZING MACHINE™ ↓

'Hello!' said the kitten. 'We've come to give you a big hug!'

Now the animals didn't know it, but Mr White was the only unlovely person in Lovelyville and he had only one thing on his evil mind that morning — who was he going to test his new PUL-VERIZING AND MASHING MACHINE™ on? He couldn't believe his good luck.

'Well,' he said, 'what a nice surprise! Won't you all please come inside?'

PLEASE COME INSIDE.

The animals went inside.

Mr White shut the door and locked it. He rubbed his hands.

'Prepare to die!' he said. He pulled a cord and a heavy black curtain parted to reveal his

145 STOP THIS MADNESS

insanely evil PULVERIZING AND
MASHING MACHINE™.

The animals gasped.

In front of them was a bath-
tub and suspended above it were
two giant pistons. On the end of
one piston was what looked like
a giant potato masher, and on
the other a giant pitchfork.

The animals were very fright-
ened.

'Who's going to be first?'
said Mr White.

The kitten gulped.

'Take me and let the others
go free!' she begged.

'And deprive me of a wonderful morning's entertainment?'
said Mr White. 'You must be mad!
I intend to pulverize and mash
all of you! And then I will turn
my PULVERIZING AND MASHING
MACHINE™ to work upon the whole
of Lovelyville! I will not be
happy until I have popped the
head of every lovely person,
mashed the petals of every

THINK
ABOUT
IT.

lovely flower and crushed every single lovely thing in this lovely, lovely land!'

And on saying this he reached out and grabbed all the animals, threw them into his machine and pressed the on button.

It was incredible. Bits and pieces of kittens, puppies and ponies went flying everywhere as the twin pulverizers and mashers went to work and the blood and guts and fur went all over Mr White and filled up the house and he drowned and then the house blew apart and a tidal wave of blood and guts flooded out over the whole town, and everybody got drowned and those who didn't got sucked into the PULVERIZING AND MASHING MACHINE™ and got pulverized and mashed, every last lovely person — every last lovely animal, every last lovely vegetable and mineral — all mashed beyond recognition, all pulverized beyond belief,

147

After all that pulverizing and mashing I think I need some really lovely hugs!

every last bit of loveliness
crushed, killed and destroyed.

And the town was renamed
BLOODYVILLE and nobody ever
went there again because the
smell was so bad that anybody
who smelt it died instantly.

The End.

I put the story down.

Danny's eyes are wide. His mouth is
frozen open. He's staring at me in horror.

'Danny?' I say. 'Danny? Are you all right?'

He can hardly talk. I've obviously really
freaked him out. He points at me.

'It's just a story, Danny,' I say. 'It didn't
really happen.'

I look closer at him.

He's not pointing at me at all. He's pointing over my shoulder.

I turn.

Oh no.

Lisa is standing behind me. She's crying.
And not just crying. I mean sobbing. Tears
are streaming down her cheeks. She must
have heard the whole thing.

DOUBLE HAMM

WE NEED TO LEARN TO TALK. SORT OUT OUR PROBLEMS.

'Those poor animals,' she sobs. 'They didn't deserve that. It was so cruel. Such a cruel, heartless thing to do.'

'Um . . . err . . . ah,' I stutter. 'It's just a story.'

I know this is a pathetic answer, but I don't know what else to say. I've blown it. Really blown it.

'Did you write it?' sobs Lisa.

What can I say? She's going to hate me if I admit it's mine. I don't want her to hate me. There's only one thing I can do. Lie.

'No,' I say. 'It's not my story.'

'It's not?' she sobs.

Danny frowns.

'But . . .' he says.

'No!' I say. 'I swear on my mother's grave that I didn't write it!'

SORRY, I CHANGED MY MIND.

'But your mother's not dead, is she?' says Lisa.

'My grandmother's grave,' I say.

'But she's not dead either,' says Danny. 'She lives in Mildura and . . .'

'Well, actually no, Danny,' I lie. 'I forgot to tell you that she died.'

'She was okay last week,' says Danny.

'It was very sudden,' I say. 'She just got sick and died. It happens, you know.'

TRIPLE HMM.

WE NEED TO UNDERSTAND EACH OTHER.

'Oh,' says Danny. 'I'm sorry.'

'So am I,' says Lisa.

'Yeah, well, never mind,' I say, 'but I swear on my grandmother's extremely freshly dug grave that I did not write that story.'

'Then if you didn't,' says Lisa. 'Who did?'

I point at Danny.

'It was him!' I say.

Danny looks alarmed.

'Me?' says Danny. 'But . . .'

Lisa turns to Danny.

Boy, he's really in for it now. Lisa loves animals.

'That's the saddest story I've ever heard,' says Lisa, her eyes shining through her tears. 'So sad, so moving . . . so cruel and yet . . . so beautiful. You're a very talented writer, Danny.'

What? She likes it? But she was crying. I thought she hated it! I'll never understand girls.

But I can't tell her that I wrote it now. I can't go back on my lie. Especially when I just swore on my grandmother's grave. I know my grandmother's not really dead, but to admit that would only make me a double liar. The only thing to do is to try and take some of the credit.

'It was my idea,' I say. 'I helped him.'

'Yeah,' says Danny. 'Andy was a big help. He practically wrote it.'

Lisa shakes her head.

'I'm sure you're just being modest,' she says. 'You were the runner-up in the school short-story competition after all.'

'I helped him with that story too,' I say.

'You did not,' says Danny, puffing his chest out. 'That was all *my* work.'

'No, it wasn't,' I say.

Lisa rolls her eyes.

'Quit messing around, Andy,' she says.

Danny looks at me and shrugs.

From Pg.90

FOR A FREE HOME TRIAL OF DR WOMKLE'S DREAM DE-NEBULIZER SEE Pg.183

'Danny,' says Lisa. 'You know that project we have to do for English where we have to write about our favourite author?'

'Yeah,' says Danny. 'What about it?'

'Well,' she says, 'I was wondering if I could do mine on you?'

Danny blushes a deep red.

'I guess so,' he stammers.

I cough. I splutter. I gag. But they ignore me.

'Great!' says Lisa, opening her notebook. 'Can I interview you? I'd love to know where you get your ideas from.'

'Well,' says Danny, sitting up in his chair and folding his arms. 'It's not that hard. You just need some sort of monster. It's not that important what it is. It can be an alien . . . or a robot . . . or even a chicken. It doesn't matter. It just has to be evil and want to destroy everything.'

NEW MOVIES PRESENT: MECHO! THE MECHANICAL CHICKEN FROM HELL!!

'Like this you mean?' I say. I raise my arms, roar like a monster and stomp towards Danny. I'm going to rip him to pieces.

Lisa touches my arm.

'Andy,' she sighs, 'you are so immature. If you're not interested in learning from someone as talented as Danny, then perhaps you could go away and leave us in peace.'

'Yes,' says Danny. 'Why don't you run along and play?'

I don't know what to say.

I put my arms down, turn and shuffle slowly towards the door.

This has got to be the lowest point of my entire life. And that's saying something.

But hold on.

I may have lost the competition.

I may have lost my dignity.

And I may have lost the best chance I've ever had to impress Lisa.

QUACK!

HOW'S THAT?

152

MMPH MPHH.

But I'm not a loser.

I'm a winner.

Because now I know exactly what sort of stories Lisa likes.

All I have to do is write another one.

I can't wait to get started on it.

I don't exactly know what's going to happen yet, but I do know it will involve bunnies, lambs, fluffy ducklings, a couple of baby seals and a maniac driving a steam-roller.

She's going to love it.

Learn to Read
with Andy

See me jump.

See me run.

See me hop.

It is fun.

See me hop.

See me run.

See me jump.

Fun, fun, fun.

See me jump.

On my bed.

I jump so high

I bump my head.

On the ceiling.

On the roof.

I hit it hard.

Ouch! Ugh! Oof!

I say a word.

It is bad.

It is rude.

I am glad.

I like to swear.

It is fun.

Bad words, rude
words.

Fun, fun, fun.

156

I AM IN CONTROL

Hop, hop, hop.

Bump, bump, bump.

Swear, swear, swear.

Jump, jump, jump.

On my tummy.

On my bum.

See me jump.

Fun, fun, fun.

157 GOOD BYE OLD FRIEND.

Hear my bed-springs.

Hear them groan.

Hear them squeak.

Hear them moan.

Squeak, squeak,

squeak.

Groan, groan, groan.

Creak, creak, creak.

Moan, moan, moan.

This is not good.

This is bad.

Mum will hear.

She'll get mad.

I'll be in trouble.

I'll be sad.

Big trouble, bad
trouble.

Bad, bad, bad.

Oh no! Oh no!

Here she comes.

Oh no! Oh no!

Here comes my mum.

Stomp! Stomp!

Stomp!

Down the hall!

I do not like this.

Not at all!

WHAT?

The door flies open.

She's mad as hell.

See her point.

Hear her yell:

'Are you jumping
on your bed?

You stupid boy!

You'll crack your
head!

'I've told you once.

I've told you twice.

It is not good.

It is not right.

You must not jump

upon your bed!

Do you understand?'

she says.

I can fib.

It is fun.

I can fib

to anyone.

I fib to Dad.

I fib to Mum.

Fib, fib, fib.

Fun, fun, fun.

See me shrug.

Hear me fib.

'But, Mum,' I say,

'I never did.

It was not me.

It was my legs.

My naughty, wicked,

jumping legs.'

See my mummy
shake her head.
See her drag me
off the bed.
Hear her say:
'That is not true.
I will have to
punish you.'

See me struggle.

See me fight.

See my mummy
hold me tight.

Being punished
is not fun.

See me bite her.

See me run.

166

See me run.

Run, run, run.

See Mum run.

Run, run, run.

See us run.

Run, run, run.

Run, run, run.

Fun, fun, fun.

Around the bedroom.

Out the door.

See the staircase!

See me fall!

Down the stairs

on my rump.

Hear me bounce.

Bump, bump, bump.

See me land.

On the floor.

See me run.

To the door.

I must get out.

I must go fast.

Mum is looking

danger-arse.

See the door.

It opens wide.

See two big legs.

They step inside.

This is not good.

This is bad.

Those big legs
belong to Dad.

I must get out.

I must get past.

I must think quick.

I must think fast.

I know what!

I'll play a game.

Dad's a tunnel.

And I'm a train!

'Look out!' I say.

'Let me through!

I'm a train.

Choo, choo, choo.'

I push my head

against his knees.

'Toot-toot,' I say.

'Open, please.'

172

See Daddy smile.

He bends down low.

'Go, little train.

Go, go, go.'

He opens his legs.

I'm almost out.

But then I hear

my mummy shout:

'Stop that boy!

Stop him now!

He must be stopped!

I don't care how!

He's jumped and
	fibbed

and fought and bit.

He must not get

away with it!'

Feel Daddy's legs
squeeze me tight.
'What's this?' he says.
'This is not right!
You should not jump.
You should not fight.
You should not fib.
You should not bite.'

See Daddy grab me
by the ear.
Hear Mummy whoop
and clap and cheer.
Hear Daddy rant, roar,
rave and boom.
See them shut me
in my room.

I'm in trouble.

I've been bad.

I sit on my bed.

I feel SAD.

But I know how

to make SAD stop.

I can jump.

I can hop.

Hop, hop, hop.

Jump, jump, jump.

Bounce, bounce,

bounce.

Bump, bump, bump.

On my tummy.

On my bum.

See me jump.

Fun, fun, fun.

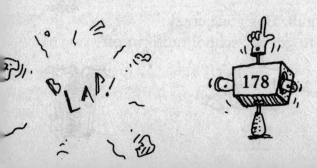

MUDMEN

I'm naked.

I'm shivering.

I'm bashing on the back door as hard as I can.

'Dad!' I yell. 'Dad! Let me in!'

I grab the door handle and push down with all my strength, but it's no use.

I must have forgotten to put the safety catch on the deadlock. What now? There's no other way into the house. All the windows are barred and the front door has an even more foolproof deadlock than the back door.

It's not my fault I'm out here with no clothes on.

It's Sooty's fault. He's gone crazy.

I came out to get my school uniform off

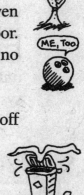

the clothesline, but it wasn't on the clothesline. It was all over the backyard. In shreds. The shreds were covered in mud—and so was Sooty. And while I was yelling at him, he stole the towel I had around my waist, ran under the porch and started ripping it to shreds as well. I'd rip him to shreds if I was small enough to get under there.

'Dad!' I yell. 'Please open the door! I'm freezing!'

Stupid Dad and his stupid deadlocks.

Ever since our house got broken into a few months ago he's gone home-security crazy. You name it, we've got it—deadlocks, bars across the windows, a closed-circuit TV surveillance system, infra-red motion detectors and a fully monitored alarm system. Not to mention a Neighbourhood Watch sticker on the letterbox.

It's a brilliant system. Dad lost the keys yesterday morning and we were trapped inside for two hours. Mum and Jen are in Mildura for the week visiting my grandparents so they couldn't help us. We had to wait until the police arrived, alerted by the alarm system.

'DAD!'

I yell even louder and bang on the door at the same time. But it's no use. He must still be in the shower. I'm going to have to go around to the bathroom window.

I go back down the steps and around the side of the house to the bathroom.

That's weird. I can't hear the shower running.

'Dad?' I call. 'Are you in there?'

He doesn't answer.

'Dad?' I call again.

'Andy?' he calls. But not from the bathroom. He's calling from around the back of the house. He must have heard me the first time. I run down the side of the house and around to the backyard. Dad's standing outside the back door, a towel around his waist.

'What are you doing?' he says. 'You're supposed to be getting ready for school—not wandering naked around the backyard!'

'It's not my fault,' I say. 'I *was* getting ready. I came outside to get my clothes off the line but Sooty has ripped them up and then he stole my towel. And then I couldn't get back inside because your deadlocks kept me out.'

Dad sucks in his breath and begins to shake his head.

'It's always somebody else's fault, isn't it?' he says. 'When are you going to start taking some responsibility for your own behaviour?'

'But it's true!' I say. 'Sooty's gone crazy!'

'Now listen here,' says Dad. 'Let's get some things straight. Sooty is not crazy . . .'

But while he is talking, Sooty emerges from underneath the porch.

'Dad!' I say.

'Don't interrupt me!' he says. 'Secondly, it is not my fault if you get locked out of the house, I've explained how to use the dead-locks . . .'

'Dad!' I say. 'Look behind you!'

'I said don't interrupt me and I meant it!' says Dad, frowning.

'But,' I say, watching Sooty get closer and closer to him. He's taking slow deliberate steps like he's stalking prey.

'Not another word!' says Dad.

Sooty strikes.

He leaps through the air and in one deft movement rips Dad's towel from around his waist.

'What the . . .?' says Dad.

He turns around, only to see Sooty disappearing underneath the porch with his towel.

Dad is standing there, nude, his mouth gaping.

'I hate to say I told you so,' I say, 'I mean, I really really really hate to say I told you so, but I . . .'

'Shut up, Andy!' says Dad. 'This is all your fault!'

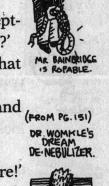

YOU'RE LATE!!

MR BAINBRIDGE IS ROPABLE.

'My fault?' I say. 'But what about accepting responsibility for your own behaviour?'

But Dad seems to have lost interest in that subject.

'Just come back inside, get dressed and get ready for school,' he says.

(FROM PG. 151)
DR. WOMKLE'S DREAM DE-NEBULIZER.

'But what am I going to wear?' I say.

'One of your sister's dresses for all I care!' he says. 'I just don't want to be late for work again. Mr Bainbridge was ropable yesterday.'

Dad stomps back up the steps.

FREE HOME TRIAL?
'HUH!
IN YOUR DREAMS!!'

'What about the door?' I say. 'Did you leave the deadlock catch off?'

'Of course I did,' says Dad. 'Think I don't know how to work a simple deadlock?'

He pushes down on the handle.

Nothing happens.

He tries it again. Still nothing.

He bangs his head against the door.

'Why me?' he says.

KNOCK.
KNOCK.

183

FOR MORE VACUUM FACTS SEE PG: 38

Bang.

'Why me?'

Bang.

'What did I do to deserve this?'

Bang.

I put my hand on his shoulder.

'Dad?' I say.

'What?' he says.

'Do you think you should be doing that to your head?' I say.

'What else is there to do?' he says.

'Um,' I say. 'Try to find another way in?'

'There is no other way in,' he says. 'The doors are double-deadlocked. The windows are barred. And even if we could prise the bars apart, the motion detectors would alert the police long before we could get in.'

'Well, why don't we do that?' I say.

Dad snorts.

'Use your head, Andy!' he says. 'We're naked. We have no way of proving who we are. They'd arrest us.'

'We could get the neighbours to vouch for us,' I say. 'They'd tell the police who we are.'

Dad stops and thinks for a moment. Then he shakes his head.

'No,' he says. 'It's bad enough to be locked

184

out of your own home, let alone having to parade around nude in front of the neighbours. I'd be a laughing stock.'

Hmmm. He's right. I don't exactly like the idea of being nude in front of the neighbours—not to mention the police—anymore than Dad does. It's bad enough being nude in front of my dad, and even worse, to have him nude in front of me.

Then I have a brainwave.

'What about the spare key?' I ask.

Dad moans. 'It used to be under the doormat, but Neighbourhood Watch say you shouldn't keep keys in such obvious places.'

'So where is it now?' I say.

Dad moans again.

'I left it at work,' he says. 'In my office.'

'We could go and get it,' I say.

'But we have no clothes on,' says Dad.

Dad has a point. But we've got to do something. I'm freezing.

I jog up and down to try and keep warm. But I slip on the wet ground and fall backwards onto the muddy lawn.

I get up.

My legs are covered in mud and little bits of grass.

JANE WAITS FOR A BUS.

POKE!

185

Hey! I've got it.

'Dad,' I say, 'I know how we can get to your work and get the key!'

'How?' he says.

'We can cover ourselves in mud and grass. It will be like camouflage.'

'Don't be stupid,' says Dad. 'This is serious.'

'I'm not being stupid,' I say. 'Watch this!'

I scoop up a big double-handful of mud and smear it across my chest. I grab another handful and rub it into my belly. I lie down on my back and roll around until I'm completely covered—from head to toe—in mud.

All the while Dad is standing there studying me like I'm something that just arrived from another planet.

'Well,' I say. 'What do you think?'

'I think you're completely insane,' says Dad.

'Yes,' I say, 'I know, but we'd only have to travel a few blocks. If we keep to backyards where possible and just move really fast across the open areas we'll be there in no time and nobody will even notice us. It's still pretty early.'

'It's a crazy plan,' he says. 'But . . .'

'But, Dad . . .' I say.

OUCH!

186

SORRY.

'Let me finish,' he says. 'I was going to say it's so crazy it just might work. Besides, I'm damned if I know what else we can do.'

'Good point!' I say. 'What have we got to lose?'

'You're right,' he says. 'Let's do it!'

He bends down and starts slopping big handfuls of mud onto himself. He breaks into a broad grin.

'Well,' he says, 'how do I look?'

'Looking good, Dad!' I say. 'Just like a regular mudman!'

The more mud he slops on, the more excited he gets. He's like a little kid. He pastes mud all over his body, and all over his head. It's in his hair, his eyes, his mouth. He looks really freaky—not like my dad at all. He covers his private parts with a leaf and hands one to me.

'Better put this on,' he says. 'Just in case.'

'Just in case what?' I say.

'In case somebody sees us,' he says.

'Nobody will see us!' I say. 'Because we're mudmen! Invisible to the eye! We travel where we want! When we want! How we want!'

'Mudmen!' says Dad, holding out his muddy hand, palm upwards. 'Give me five!'

TYPES OF LEAVES FOR COVERING YOUR PRIVATE PARTS WITH.

I give him five. Mud splashes out from our hands. I haven't seen Dad this excited since . . . since . . . well, actually I've never seen him this excited.

The sky is filled with dark clouds. That's good. It makes it less likely that we'll be seen.

We climb up our fence and into Mr Broadbent's yard. Crouching low we run across the yard and climb over his fence.

'So far, so good!' says Dad, as we run across the second yard and scale the next fence.

We drop down into the third backyard. There's plenty of cover here. It's full of trees and shrubs.

'Too easy!' giggles Dad.

'See, I told you!' I say.

We continue on our way, leaping fences like they're nothing more than hurdles in a hundred-metre dash.

Wooden fences, galvanised iron, high-security fences—nothing stops us. We're mudmen!

We thread our way through compost heaps, swimming pools and veggie gardens. All the while getting more and more caked in mud and leaves and dirt.

We stop, panting, in the last backyard in our street.

'I haven't had this much fun since I was in the boy scouts!' says Dad, wheezing.

'You covered yourselves in mud and ran around the streets in boy scouts?' I say.

'No,' he laughs. 'We went bushwalking and orienteering—but this is much better!'

'Okay,' I say. 'We're going to have to run down the side of this house and cross the road to the house opposite to get to the next set of backyards. Are you ready?'

'Ready!' says Dad.

We run down the side of the house and cross the footpath to the nature-strip.

Oh no!

There's a car coming out of the driveway of the house beside us.

There's no time to hide.

'What do we do now?' says Dad.

'Freeze!' I say. 'Put your hands out to your side. We'll pretend we're trees!'

We both stop dead and put our arms out at weird angles.

'I don't think we look much like trees,' whispers Dad out of the side of his mouth.

He's right, but it doesn't seem to matter.

REX STROMSKI'S WALK TO WORK NAKED BACKWARDS!

ARGH!

SPLAT!!

KNOCK KNOCK

189

The driver of the car doesn't even give us a second glance as he pulls out onto the road and takes off.

'Phew, that was close,' says Dad.

'But we did it!' I say.

'Yeah!' he says, his muddy eyes shining. 'We did it!'

He runs across the road and leaps over the low brick fence that runs along the front of the house on the corner. I follow him, down the side of the house, into the backyard and over the fence.

Dad's really moving now. I have to run as fast as I can to keep up with him.

As I'm climbing over a tall green fence I see him standing in the middle of a yard under a clothesline. He's holding a large pair of jeans above his head. I drop down into the yard and join him.

'Look what I found!' he says. 'This should make things easier!'

'Great, Dad,' I say. 'But let's keep moving. Before someone sees us.'

Dad is bending over, trying to put the jeans on.

Out of the corner of my eye I notice something move.

190

I hear growling.

Uh-oh.

I quickly review how many yards we've been through and I realise what backyard we're in . . . the backyard of number 19. The home of the bull terrier.

It comes running across the grass towards Dad.

'Forget the jeans, Dad,' I say. 'Run!'

I head towards the fence. The bull terrier follows me, baring its teeth and snarling. I start climbing the fence, the bull terrier snapping at my legs.

Dad runs towards us. He twirls the jeans around and flicks them like they're a rolled up tea-towel. He hits the dog on its back. It turns and attacks him.

Dad grabs the bull terrier around the stomach and wrestles it to the ground. They roll around together in the mud. Fighting, thrashing and growling. It's hard to tell who's growling the loudest. It's incredible. I've never seen Dad like this before. It's like watching Tarzan wrestle with a leopard.

Dad looks up at me.

'What are you waiting for?' he yells. 'Go!'

But I can't. I can't tear myself away. The bull

terrier is winning. It's on top of Dad, its fangs bared, ready to sink them into Dad's neck.

'No!' I scream.

THERE ARE NO DRAWINGS ON THIS PAGE.

But then in one amazingly fast movement, Dad reaches up, grabs the dog's neck, clamps its jaws shut with his hand and wraps the jeans around its muzzle and head. He ties the legs of the jeans in a knot and pulls them tight.

IT IS NAKED!

Dad leaps up onto the fence and swings his legs over onto the other side. The dog is staggering around the backyard, blinded by the jeans, furiously trying to shake them off its head. It crashes into a tree and falls over.

I drop down and join Dad.

'That was brilliant, Dad!' I say. 'Shame you had to give up your jeans, though.'

Dad is wired, electric, alive.

(OR WOULD BE IF THIS WRITING EXPLAINING THAT IT IS NAKED WASN'T HERE.)

'Doesn't matter,' he says, beaming. 'What do I need with jeans, anyway? I'm a MUDMAN!'

Mudman? He looks more like a madman. His hair's all stiff with mud and sticking out at crazy angles. His eyes are wide and white and he's got blood dripping from a wound on his shoulder where the bull terrier must have bitten him. He looks wild.

'Come on,' he says. 'We've got to keep moving.'

IRON GLOVE WHO?

192

I can't believe how much Dad's got into this. It's like he's not even my dad anymore.

We make it through the next five back-yards without any problems. We jump over the last fence into a laneway.

'Not far now!' says Dad.

WATER-
MELON

We sprint along the lane as fast as we can. At the end of the lane we flatten our backs against a wall. We look out across a busy highway. The traffic is bumper to bumper.

NAKED
WATER-
MELON.

Dad's work is on the other side of the road. There is a factory, a warehouse and a two-storey office block. Dad's office is on the second floor.

'We're almost there,' says Dad. 'All we have to do is cross the road.'

'Hang on,' I say. 'Just one question. How do we get to your office? We can't exactly go through reception.'

'But we're mudmen!' he says. 'We can go anywhere we want!'

'But not through reception,' I say. 'Think about it.'

Dad thinks.

'You're right,' he says. 'Mrs Lewis might have a heart attack.'

We stand in the lane and study the buildings.

193

NOT IRONGLOVE!
EYE AND GLOVE!

We're so close, and yet, so far.

I really thought we were going to make it.

It's hard to believe that we've come all this way for nothing.

Suddenly Dad grabs my arm.

THE ANTI-
NAKEDNESS
COMMITTEE
'PANTS ON'
CAMPAIGN.

JUST
CRAZY

BOOKS.

'I've got it!' he says. 'See that shed near the fence?' He points to a small grey building just inside the gate.

I nod.

'What about it?' I say.

ART.

'It's a maintenance shed,' he says. 'They keep overalls in there. We can put them on and go and get the key. No problem. No heart attacks. Let's go.'

The cars are still bumper to bumper.

TRANSPORT.

'Hang on,' I say. 'Are we just going to run across the road? Shouldn't we wait until there's a break in the traffic?'

MEDIA.

'It'll be like this for another hour at least,' says Dad. 'We haven't got time. Just keep your eyes straight ahead and don't look back!'

I look at him.

He pats me on the back.

'Come on, mudboy,' he says. 'You can do it.'

I put my hands up on either side of my face like blinkers. If I can't see them, they can't see me.

WHAT?

194

EYE.
GLOVE.

We thread our way through the cars.

People are yelling and hooting and honking their horns.

They've obviously never seen mudmen before.

Dad is just in front of me, moving quickly through the traffic. We come to a four-wheel drive that is parked so close to the car in front we can't get through. Dad leaps over the bonnet in one bound. I take my hands away from my face and follow him.

'Andy?' says a voice, as I clamber across the front of the car.

I look at the driver.

Oh no.

It's my teacher, Ms Livingstone.

'Hi,' I say. 'I know this looks a bit strange, but . . .'

She raises her hand and smiles.

'Not to me,' she says. 'I spent six months living with the Mud-people of Papua New Guinea. I'll never forget it. There was this one time . . .'

Uh-oh. Ms Livingstone's travel stories are fascinating, but once she gets started she can go on for hours.

'I'd love to hear about it sometime, Ms

Livingstone,' I say, 'but I'm kind of in a hurry right now.'

She smiles and nods.

A NAKED MECHANICAL CHICKEN.

'I understand,' she says. 'That's exactly how the Mud-people were—never still, always rushing here and there. I remember one time . . .'

I slide off the bonnet and keep running.

We reach the other side of the road and sprint along the fence to the front gates of Dad's work.

There's nobody around. That's good.

We cut across to the maintenance shed.

Dad tries to open the door.

It's locked. That's bad.

'Damn!' says Dad, slamming his fist on the door. 'The caretaker usually has this unlocked by now.'

He steps back from the door and looks at the shed.

GEE! IT'S COLD.

MUDMEN. FIRST PEOPLE TO CLIMB MT EVEREST NAKED. (EXCEPT FOR THIN LAYER OF MUD.)

'What are we going to do now?' he says. 'We're doomed!'

'No, we're not, Dad,' I say. 'We're mudmen, remember? We can do anything!'

'We're not mudmen,' he says. 'We're just a couple of naked morons covered in mud. I should have known this wouldn't work. I

EYE. GLOVE EYE GLOVE

should never have listened to you. What on earth was I thinking?'

I look at Dad. Something has changed. A few minutes ago he was running through the streets without his clothes on, leaping over cars and fences, and fighting dogs with his bare hands. Now he's staring at me with wide desperate eyes. I have to take over.

I turn away from Dad and study the shed.

There's a set of louvre windows above the door.

'Maybe I can get in through there,' I say. 'I could slide out the glass and climb through.'

'But how are you going to get up there?' says Dad.

'On your shoulders,' I say. 'Crouch down.'

Dad crouches and looks around nervously.

'Okay,' he says. 'But hurry. People will be arriving any minute now.'

I put one foot on his mud-caked shoulders. The mud is half dried and gives my foot plenty of grip. I grab Dad's right hand and pull myself up onto his other shoulder. I grab his left hand and steady myself.

'Okay,' I say. 'I'm ready.'

Dad stands up and I rise up to the level of the window.

I let go of his hand and try to remove the first pane of glass. It's not easy though. It won't budge. I try to loosen it by rattling it and it moves a little, but not much.

'I can't get it,' I call down to Dad. 'It's stuck.'

'Try the next one up,' he says. 'Hurry!'

I try it. Much better. It slides out smoothly. I place the glass on the gutter above me and start work on the next one. It slides out easily too.

I go back to the first bit of glass.

It's still stuck.

I feel a drop of water on my head.

And another.

I look up.

Uh-oh. It's starting to rain.

Just what we didn't need.

There is an enormous clap of thunder. The clouds open up properly and the first few drops give way to the most incredible downpour. It's like the cloud above us has been holding on for weeks, months—possibly years. But not anymore. Down it comes. Right on top of us. On top of our mud. And begins to wash it away.

'Hurry up, Andy!' says Dad.

198

'I'm trying to!' I yell. 'But the window is stuck.'

'Just break it!' pleads Dad. 'I'll replace it later! We have to get those overalls!'

I can hardly see anything. The mud is washing off my hair and into my eyes. It must be even worse for Dad because all my mud is washing off me and down onto him. I wipe my eyes and try to work out how to break the window.

I'm just about to karate chop it when I hear a noise. A car is pulling up alongside us.

I look over my shoulder.

Uh-oh.

It's Mr Bainbridge. Dad's boss.

He's getting out of the passenger side of the car.

The car is being driven by Mrs Bainbridge.

'Andy?' says Mr Bainbridge.

'Who is that?' says Dad, turning around to see.

'No!' I scream. 'Don't turn around!'

But it's too late.

I teeter on his shoulders as he turns. Dad puts his hands up to steady me. I grab them.

'Aagghh!' says Mr Bainbridge.

WORLD-WIDE GO TO WORK NAKED DAY.

THE POPE JOINS IN.

AMERICAN PRESIDENTS LIKE IT.

THE QUEEN GETS IT ALL OFF.

BUT, WHERE DO I KEEP MY WALLET?

199

'Aagghh!' says Dad.

'Cover your eyes, dear!' yells Mr Bainbridge, running around to the driver's side of the car to stand in front of Mrs Bainbridge's window.

MR BAINBRIDGE SUDDENLY REALISES HE HAS TURNED UP TO WORK NAKED.

BUT IT IS NOT WORLD GO TO WORK NAKED DAY.

Now don't get me wrong, but I'm not too worried about the Bainbridges seeing *me* in the nude. It's happened so many times now that it's almost routine, but I feel for Dad. This is his first time ever.

'So this is where he gets it from,' says Mr Bainbridge. 'Like father, like son!'

'I'm very sorry, Mr Bainbridge,' says Dad. 'I know this seems highly irregular but I can assure you there is a very good reason . . .'

Mr Bainbridge puts up his hand.

'Don't waste my time and your breath,' he says. 'As you well know I am a man of high standards and I demand the same from my employees. I do not expect to come to work and find them naked, covered in mud and performing acrobatics in the driveway. I've come to expect this sort of behaviour from your feral son, but for a man of your age and in your position it is inexcusable! I will not tolerate it. You are fired.'

'But Mr Bainbridge,' splutters Dad. 'I . . . I . . . I . . .'

Poor Dad. He's struggling here. He's obviously not as used to making up excuses as I am.

'It's okay, Dad,' I say. 'I'll handle this.'

I look down at Mr Bainbridge.

'You can't fire my dad!' I say.

'And why not?' says Mr Bainbridge.

'Because this isn't really happening,' I say.

'Not happening?' says Mr Bainbridge. 'What are you talking about?'

'It's a hallucination,' I say. 'You've been working very hard lately. We're just products of your confused mind. You should get back in the car, go home and have a good long lie-down . . .'

'That'll do, Andy,' says Dad.

'Don't listen to him, Mr Bainbridge,' I yell. 'He's a hallucination. He doesn't know what he's talking about.'

'No, Andy,' says Dad, 'no more lies.'

Dad bends down and lowers me to the ground. He stands up straight, and faces Mr Bainbridge.

'Mr Bainbridge,' he says, 'I don't mind at all that you've fired me, because you've just saved me the trouble of quitting.'

Mr Bainbridge gasps in shock. So do I.

201

And so does Mrs Bainbridge, who is peeking out from behind Mr Bainbridge.

'You see,' says Dad, 'I realised something about myself this morning. I realised that I've been living a half-life. A safe life. A boring life. A life of too much responsibility and not enough fun. Not enough danger.'

What is Dad on about? Obviously the stress of being locked out of his house without any clothes on has driven him over the edge.

CRAZY FOR LIFE.

CHIRP

'Dad,' I say, 'do you know what you're saying? Are you crazy?'

'Yes,' says Dad, putting his arm around my shoulders. 'I'm crazy all right. Crazy for life! I want to take more chances, climb more mountains, swim more rivers and watch more sunsets. Life's too short to waste, Andy. You, me, Mum and Jen—we're going to escape this ratrace. We're going to leave the city. We're going to live off the land—in the wild—in the raw.'

'We are?!' I say.

'Yes,' says Dad, sweeping his arm through the air. 'We don't need all . . . this! Come on, son, let's get out of here.'

'But, Dad,' I say, 'what about the overalls?'

Dad kneels down and picks up a fresh

handful of mud and starts slapping it all over himself.

'Overalls?' he says. 'Who needs overalls when we've got mud?'

'But the key,' I say. 'We haven't got the key.'

'We don't need a key,' he says. 'We'll climb onto the roof and go down the chimney like we should have done in the first place! It'll be a challenge. And, more importantly, it will be fun!'

He slaps a few more handfuls of mud carelessly across his body and marches off down the drive, not even looking back.

It's stopped raining. The clouds have broken up and golden rays of light illuminate my dad, highlighting every muscle in his body. He looks stronger than I ever imagined he could.

Mr and Mrs Bainbridge are just staring, slack-jawed.

I give them a shrug and run after my dad. Well, what else can I do?

I'm a little worried about how our new life is going to work exactly, and what Mum and Jen are going to think about it when they get back home, but speaking for myself, I think it sounds kind of fun.

Crazy, but fun.

Also available from Macmillan Children's Books

Andy Griffiths
Illustrated by Terry Denton

Just Kidding!

In *Just Annoying!* Andy established himself as the world's most annoying person. But did you realize that he is also the world's leading practical joker? The ten hilarious stories in *Just Kidding!* show case Andy's skills as a class-one prankster— the only problem is that his jokes usually end up backfiring!

In 'Playing Dead' Andy pretends that he is dead to get out of going to school, but when his parents prepare to bury him in the backyard he starts to wonder if it was such a clever idea after all. Other practical jokes include pretending that corn relish is puke to make an old lady move seats on a plane, and dressing up as a gorillagram to embarrass his sister, Jen, at her birthday party.

Andy Griffiths
Illustrated by Terry Denton

Just Annoying!

There is a fine line between playing tricks on people and annoying the heck out of them. Andy should know. He crosses the line on a regular basis!

In *Just Annoying!* nine unique stories find Andy in hilarious situations such as setting a new speed record by swinging on the clothes line, being terrorized by a garden gnome that he has taken on holiday with him, chasing the last Jaffa in the cinema and having his imaginary friends taking on a life of their own.

Andy Griffiths
Illustrated by Terry Denton

Just Stupid!

Gasp as Andy careers down a hill in an abandoned pram wearing only a nappy, *groan* as he desperately looks for a toilet in a shopping centre before he explodes, and *squirm* as he stuffs twenty marshmallows into his mouth without swallowing . . .

But most of all *laugh* because Andy is back—and doing more stupid things than ever before.

Nine original stories that see Andy G lurch from one stupid mistake to another.

Morris Gleitzman

Blabber Mouth

Two hours ago, when I walked into the school for the first time, the sun was shining, the birds were singing and, apart from a knot in my guts the size of Tasmania, life was great.

Now here I am, locked in the stationery cupboard.

Rowena wants to be friends but the other kids don't.

It is because she's just stuffed a frog into Darryn Peck's mouth? Or is it because of her dad? How can she tell him that his shirts, and his habit of singing in public, are wrecking her life?

It's not easy—especially when you can't speak.

This first hilarious and heartwarming story about Rowena Batts from one of Australia's funniest children's authors.

Tim Winton

Lockie Leonard, Human Torpedo

Mrs Leonard came in, twitchy and nervous. She laid a little green book on the bed and looked out of the window. 'It's time we thought about sex,' she said.

But Lockie can hardly think about anything else . . . New in town, and not exactly riding high in the popularity stakes, Lockie suddenly discovers the gorgeous green-eyed girl who sits at the front of his maths class—and who, miraculously, likes him!

Suddenly Lockie is famous for more than just his hot-shot surfing. Suddenly he is in love with the most fabulous girl in the school. And no booklet in the world could have prepared him for that!

Tim Winton

Lockie Leonard, Scum Buster

Lockie Leonard, for the second time in his life, felt himself dragged kicking and screaming into the twilight zone. Aaarrrghhh! It couldn't be true. But it was. He was barking-mad, brain-dead, leglessly in love.

Lockie Leonard's life is a disaster area.

His new best friend is probably the oddest human being on Planet Earth.

His bid to save the town from industrial pollution has run into the apathy zone.

And now, just to round things off, he's gone and fallen for a kid who's still in primary school. And she even surfs better than him!

Can things get worse?

Of course they can.

Lockie Leonard, Human Torpedo, is about to crash!

The hilarious sequel to *Lockie Leonard, Human Torpedo*.

Tim Winton

Lockie Leonard, Legend

Lockie started to run. I'm a fool, he thought, a mad, insane, lunatic idiot. I should be locked up and fed dog biscuits. I'm a damned disgrace.

Lockie's life is crumbling. His best friend has left town. He's had his first big love disaster. His mum won't stop crying. His baby sister can't stop filling her nappy—and guess who's got to change it?

Things can't get any worse. Really, they can't. Unless you happen to be Lockie Leonard. In which case, disaster on a legendary scale is just around the corner . . .